CHRISTMAS
in
BEAUFORT

Christmas in Beaufort

First Edition.
ISBN-13: 978-0-692-40577-2
ISBN-10: 0-692-40577-1

Copy edited by Marcus Trower.

www.adamfletcherseries.com
www.sarawhitford.com

SEAPORT
PUBLISHING

Merry Christmas.

CHRISTMAS
in
BEAUFORT

Sara Whitford

Chapter One

THE MILD NOVEMBER DAYS THE residents of New Bern were enjoying lately provided a welcome time of rest for Adam Fletcher and the companions of his most recent series of journeys. They had taken him from Beaufort to Boston, with a number of unexpected and highly stressful stops along the way.

He knew his family would be worrying about him back in Beaufort. He also couldn't help but wonder how his father had fared on his own leg of the journey. After dropping Adam and Will off in Edenton, Santiago had gone much farther south—towards Havana—and he was sailing with a reduced crew, since several of his sailors had attempted mutiny on the return trip from Boston. They would be held in confinement on board *La Dama* until they could be turned over to the authorities in Cuba. Adam had gotten no indication from his father about if or when he'd be back to Beaufort.

If it weren't for the absolute exhaustion Adam and the others felt after their recent ordeal, along with the fresh scars on Adam's back from the lashes he had recently received, they would have likely already left for Carteret County with Laney and Aunt Celie.

As it was, however, Dr. Beasley, a kindhearted old physician, was checking in each day to look after Adam, specifically to make sure his wounds weren't at risk of infection. He recommended that Adam stay put for at least a few days to give his injuries a chance to scab over well, and that he not risk possibly being caught in rain or other circumstances that could interfere with the healing.

Saturday morning after the night Adam, Will, and Charles Jr. arrived back in New Bern, Adam was taken by surprise while he was sitting in the parlor reading the most recent newspaper from a stack of them that Will had picked up from a neighbor. Laney and Aunt Celie came into the room and insisted he remove his shirt and lie down on the settee so they could examine his wounds and clean and dress them.

Dr. Beasley arrived as they were finishing up. When he saw what they had done, he commended the women on doing a fine job of cleaning the lash marks. "It'll make my job a good bit easier," he said.

Adam was still stretched out on his belly, his head resting on his arms. He tried his best to see what the doctor was doing.

"Laney, why don't you take that out back so Dr. Beasley will have room to work?" Will suggested. He was referring to the basin Laney and Aunt Celie had used. It was still on the table next to the settee.

She nodded and took the basin and rags out of the room.

The old man sat in a chair that had been pulled right beside the settee and opened up his medical bag. It contained small bottles of a variety of tinctures that Adam couldn't begin to identify. However, he ended up taking out a jar of a substance that *did* look familiar to Adam.

"Is that honey?" he asked.

"Mm-hm," Dr. Beasley replied as he took some cloth strips out of his bag and draped the bundle in a pile at the small of Adam's back—the only area of flesh not covered in angry red stripes.

The doctor turned and looked at Aunt Celie. "I forgot to bring a spoon. Go get a spoon for me, please."

Aunt Celie gave him a nod and said, "Yessir," and then went into the dining room to find a spoon. She brought it back to him, and then she excused herself to tend to other work.

Dr. Beasley plunked the spoon down into the jar and began applying honey directly to the wounds on Adam's back. He only spread it on the areas where the skin was visibly broken. There were some welts where one could see that he had been struck, but the skin was intact. The doctor wouldn't worry about those, but across the broad, muscular part of Adam's back and his shoulders there were several places that had been torn by the whip, and they looked like they were beginning to show signs of infection.

"Are you just going to leave it like that?" Adam asked as he felt the sticky substance getting slathered onto his skin. It did burn a little bit—but then again, anything touching those cuts would've burned.

"I'll be covering the honey with these bandages. The honey is sticky, of course, so the bandages should stay in place. Do you have a clean shirt?"

"Hmm..." Adam wasn't sure what to say. He looked over

at Will, who was standing by the door that led to the foyer. Of course he didn't have a clean shirt. When he began his travels a month ago, he didn't expect to be gone longer than overnight.

He definitely didn't bring many changes of clothes.

Will said, "I have something clean he can wear."

"Well," said Dr. Beasley as he applied the last bandage, "you'll want to put on a clean shirt to keep all of this covered."

Adam nodded. "Alright."

"Try to keep everything dry," said the doctor. "I suppose after a day or two we'll know if it's time to remove them. We'll have to wait and see how they're healing up."

The doctor put the jar of honey and a couple of leftover bandages back in his bag and stood from his chair. "Well, I suppose we're finished here," he said. "I'll come back to check on you tomorrow."

Adam rose from the settee. He shook the doctor's hand and thanked him for coming by and tending to him. The old physician excused himself and left.

Adam felt a bit awkward, standing there while he waited with a back full of uncomfortable sticky bandages. He glanced across the room and noticed Laney standing near the door to the hallway. When his eyes met hers, she blushed and said, "Oh, I was just looking for Will."

Just then Aunt Celie called to her from somewhere down the hall. "Your brother's done gone upstairs to fetch a shirt for Mr. Adam," she said.

"Oh? Good! Thank you," she called back in response. "I'll go find him, then." She smiled at Adam and then disappeared down the hall, heading towards the stairs.

Adam suspected the girl wasn't looking for her brother,

but he figured she was clever for trying that excuse, anyway. He was also amused that Aunt Celie was evidently watching her like a hawk.

One thing was certain: things had definitely changed between him and Laney. He wondered how they would be once they were all back in Beaufort.

He remembered what his father and Martin had said to him about letting her know of his intentions, but he still didn't think there was any need to do that anytime soon. What would be the point?

And speaking of Martin, he wondered what had happened with him and Jenny Green… and Hardy's brothers.

Well, one thing was certain: there would be plenty of catching up to do when they all got back home.

BY THE FOLLOWING MONDAY, ADAM and his Martin family companions were getting loaded up into the periauger to travel back to Beaufort. Will decided to come along because Adam had mentioned Emmanuel's sloop, the *Carolina Gypsy*, might be making a trip north soon, and he could travel with the crew back towards Boston to rejoin his wife and baby before Christmas.

Given recent events, since Will would be leaving with Adam, Laney, and Aunt Celie, it was decided by all that it would be a good idea if Charles Jr. and Annabelle went to Beaufort with them. Although no one came right out and said it, Adam knew everyone was concerned about leaving the young couple alone at the Martin estate in New Bern—at least so soon after Annabelle's kidnapping and Charles Jr.'s imprisonment.

It was a real possibility that the Sangers, or Byrd, or even that awful Edenton constable had an ax to grind with them. No one mentioned it, though. Instead, Will and Laney insisted Charles Jr. and Annabelle come with them, because after all, it would be good for Aunt Celie to have her son and daughter-in-law with her for Christmas, which was now just weeks away.

The boat ride home would be slightly more crowded than usual, but fortunately, the vessel was plenty big to carry several more people, if needed. On the bright side, there would be plenty to talk about, so the full day-and-night's journey back to Beaufort would go by quickly.

THEY ARRIVED BACK IN BEAUFORT on Sunday morning with no fanfare, no celebration. After all, no one knew they were coming. They all decided to take Laney, Aunt Celie, Annabelle, and Charles Jr. to Laney's estate, at Lennoxville Point, before Adam and Will sailed back into town.

Once they arrived at Laney's dock, the men helped the women out of the boat and then carried all of their luggage into the house. Just as they finished getting things inside, Adam and Will stood on the back porch and were about to leave when Aunt Celie offered to fix something for everyone to eat. Will looked at Adam. Adam checked his pocket watch.

"It's only quarter to ten. I reckon everyone's at church right now, anyway," said Adam. "They won't be out for a while yet."

"That would be great, Aunt Celie," said Will.

Adam and Will went back into the house with the others, and Aunt Celie and Annabelle quickly exited out the back door and crossed the yard over to the servants' cabin, where Cyrus and Violet lived with their baby. They tended to the livestock on Laney's estate, and Cyrus helped with little repairs and maintenance around the place—like Charles Jr. had always done at Will's place in New Bern.

Adam assumed the women were going to get some eggs and some ham or bacon to fix for everyone. Since Laney and Aunt Celie had planned to be in Boston with Will and his wife's family until the spring, there were no food stores ready in the house when they arrived.

Meanwhile, Charles Jr. put some wood in the kitchen fireplace and got a roaring fire going, and he brought in some water for the women to use when they were cooking.

Within an hour, Aunt Celie and Annabelle had fixed up a big pot of grits with some scrambled eggs and bacon.

Laney, Will, and Adam ate in the dining room. Aunt Celie, Charles Jr., and Annabelle ate in the kitchen, with Annabelle coming in to check on whether Adam or the Martins needed anything a couple of times during the meal.

Will and Adam briefly discussed when Emmanuel might have the *Carolina Gypsy* scheduled to make another shipment north. Will was anxious to leave Beaufort and get back to Boston so he could be with Catherine and their baby as soon as possible. Adam told Will he seemed to remember there would be a shipment leaving in the near future for at least as far north as Philadelphia.

Adam told Laney not to worry, that he'd look after her when her brother was gone.

Will said, "Indeed, I'm going to be counting on him to keep you all safe from any unsavory characters."

Adam noticed that Laney didn't seem to have much of

an appetite, as she spent much of the meal just moving her fork around on the plate while taking only the smallest bites of food.

"You alright?" Adam asked her.

Laney raised her eyebrows in surprise. "Me? Yes, of course. Why?"

Adam shrugged. "Well, because I've noticed you've not eaten much. You seem distracted. You feeling sick?"

Laney shook her head. "No. I guess I'm just not that hungry. I think I'm probably just tired."

Will said nothing. He looked at Laney, then at Adam, then back at Laney, and then he smiled and ate another forkful of scrambled eggs mixed in with grits.

"You might not be so tired if you ate something," said Adam.

Laney sighed hard and fast. She almost looked cross as she took a sip of her tea, and then she put her napkin on the table. "I think I just need to lie down. I'll have something to eat later." She directed her attention to her brother. "Maybe you could ask Aunt Celie to make me some ginger cookies."

Will nodded. "Sure. I'll do it."

Laney excused herself from the table, and Adam could soon hear her going up the stairs.

Adam wrinkled his eyebrows. "What do you think is wrong with her?" he asked Will.

Will shrugged. "She's probably just tired."

"I don't know. She almost looked mad just before she left the table. You didn't notice?"

Will shook his head. "No, I can't say that I did. And anyway, women are a mystery."

That was no secret to Adam. He was raised by a single

mother, so perhaps they weren't as mysterious to him as they were to some men, but he was a little concerned about Laney's seemingly sudden change in mood. After all, they were *all* tired. They had *all* been on a periauger all night and all day the previous day. *None* of them had gotten much sleep, but it was also true that *none* of them had eaten much of anything, and a hot cooked meal should be welcome by *all* of them. The only thing that had even been discussed before she excused herself was that her brother was anxious to get back to Boston.

Maybe she wanted to go back with him. Maybe now she was regretting coming back to Beaufort.

Chapter Two

AROUND NOONTIME, ADAM AND WILL left in the peri-auger to Rogers's Shipping Company. Emmanuel and Boaz had already returned from church by the time the two arrived.

After receiving a hearty welcome in the upstairs living quarters, Will told Emmanuel about his desire to return to Boston. Emmanuel said they'd gotten back just in time, since the *Gypsy* was leaving on Thursday for Philadelphia.

Adam decided to leave the two of them to chat about the particulars of how that might happen, and he asked if he could take Rex to go visit Martin. His grandfather nodded and told him, "Of course, but just don't get lost on any adventures between here and there."

Adam smiled and bade them farewell, then left for Martin's house.

"GOOD GOD ALMIGHTY!" MARTIN EXCLAIMED as he answered Adam's knock at his front door. He was clearly stunned. "I was beginnin to wonder if you were dead."

Adam laughed and gave Martin's hand an animated shake. "Nah, I'm still here."

"Well, come on in here!" Martin motioned for him to come inside the house. "Sit down. We've got some catchin up to do."

They both went over to the table and sat down.

"You get back today?" Martin asked.

Adam shook his head. "Yep. This morning—while y'all were at church, actually. Had to drop off your cousin and the others first, then Will and I—"

"Wait, Laney's here? And the others? Who's here?" He stood from his seat, walked over to the cupboard, took out a bottle, and offered Adam a drink.

Adam shook his head. "Uh-uh. I'll have some cider, though, if you have it."

Martin nodded and proceeded to pour a glass for Adam from a different corked bottle.

Once they both had their drinks and were sitting at the table, Adam explained. "Will and Aunt Celie are here, and also Charles Jr. and Annabelle."

"What about Catherine and the baby?" Martin asked, inquiring about Will's wife and new son.

"Oh, they stayed in Boston. The trip would've been too much for them, but Will's going back as soon as he can secure passage, and it turns out that'll probably be later this week."

Martin nodded. "I see. Did everything go alright on the trip back down south?"

Since Adam knew that Martin would have at least heard the rough details about what took them to Boston in the first place, he didn't have to explain that part. As for the return journey, however, Adam just didn't feel like going into all of those details right now, including the full story of what happened with Charles Jr. and Annabelle. Right now, Adam was in the mood for a lighter topic.

"It's a long story, but you tell me," said Adam. "What happened after I left?"

Martin leaned back in his chair and smiled. "Which part?"

"Last I remember, I was trying to get you to hold off on going to see Jenny Greene, but I know you had your mind made up on going. So what ended up happening?"

Martin leaned forward and rested his elbows on the table, and he grinned broadly. "You'll never believe it if I tell you."

Adam raised his eyebrows, his curiosity piqued. "Oh really?"

"Me and Jenny are gettin married!" Martin scratched his head through his curly blond hair as though he almost couldn't believe the news himself.

Adam's jaw dropped and his eyes grew enormous. "Do what?!"

Martin nodded, then leaned back in his chair again and took another sip of his drink. "Yes, sir. Oh, I prob'ly waited near 'bout a week after you left before I got the word that she was back home, but I went right over to see her—she was *real* glad to see me—and we talked and talked and talked. I told her she didn't have no reason to be alone, and we need to quit messin around and just go on and get married."

"You did this?" Adam asked. "Just like that." He snapped his fingers. "You told her you wanted to get married after talking to her *one single day*. And she said yes? Is that what you're saying?" He honestly couldn't believe Martin had decided to tie the knot. He'd never liked being tied to anything or anybody.

Martin gave a half shrug, then nodded. "Well, pretty much that's how it happened."

"And you're getting married?" said Adam, bewildered. "Actually *married*? Rings and 'till death do us part' and all of that? Married?"

"Uh-huh." Martin nodded again, this time more slowly, but then he nodded once more, as if he realized that last nod might not have been convincing enough. "Yes, yes, married!"

"When?" Adam asked. "I mean, if your mind's made up, what are you waiting for? Neither of your parents are still living. I don't reckon there's a big wedding to plan or anything, right? Just go on to Reverend Miller so he can publish the banns and that's it, right?"

Martin sighed. "Well, see, that's the problem. I've been hopin you'd hurry up and get back. I was wonderin if you might just ask your grandfather to be my bondsman so we don't have to do it that way."

Adam looked at Martin as though he'd suddenly grown a second nose. "Huh? If you wanted him to be your bondsman, why haven't you asked him yet? He may be my grandfather, but for goodness' sake, you've known him years longer than I have!"

Martin didn't respond right away.

Adam furrowed his brow. "Is there something you're leaving out of this whole thing?"

"Well…" Martin dug the ball of his foot into the floor, and he seemed to be trying to think about what to say. "Well, I don't know if it'll work the other way."

Adam gave him a confused look. "You don't know if it'll work *what* way?"

"Publishin the banns, I mean."

"What? Martin Smith, you're not making a lick of sense. What do you mean, you don't know if it'll work the other way? It's worked that way for centuries, hasn't it? Why wouldn't it work for you? It's simple. Y'all go and tell Reverend Miller you want to get married. He'll announce the banns during church for three Sundays in a row, then that's it. He'll finalize the marriage and you'll be husband and wife. So how is it that it might not work for you?"

"Damnit, Adam. Think about it. Why do they read the banns?"

"I reckon there are a few reasons." Adam raised his hand and began to count them off one by one on his fingers. "First, to make sure neither of you have a spouse still living that doesn't know you're trying to get married. To make sure neither of you have some other legal impediment that should keep you from getting married—like being wanted for some crime or something. And then to make sure you're not close relatives or anything. I don't think any of those apply. Do you? I don't think there'll be a problem."

"Don't they say something like, 'Blah, blah, blah... If any of you know cause or just impediment why these two persons should not be joined together in holy matrimony, please declare it'?"

Adam nodded. "Yes. I think that's almost exactly what they say."

"And they say it on three Sundays in a row!"

"Yep."

"Well, I reckon 'cause or just impediment' could cover

a whole bunch of things, don't you? What if someone has somethin against me and just doesn't want me and Jenny to be happy? Or what if one of my old flames pops up and claims somethin about me that isn't true? Or that *is* true, but that I just don't know about?"

Adam closed his eyes, shook his head, and sighed.

He looked at Martin with complete seriousness. "I don't think you'll have to worry about any of that, but if something does come up, I'm afraid to say that poor decisions can yield poor consequences. So I reckon you just better pray it doesn't happen."

"And if it does?"

"You'll just have to cross that bridge when you get to it."

"You don't understand. We can't let *anything* get in the way of us gettin married."

"Well, if something else comes up, you might just have to work through that before you can be husband and wife."

"We don't want to have to work through anything. We want to get married now."

Adam stood in frustration. He considered leaving.

"Listen, Martin," Adam said, lightly slapping his hand down on the table where Martin sat, "you of all people ought to know that life doesn't always go exactly the way we want it to. If it was so damned important for you to marry Jenny, then why have you waited to do anything about it?"

"You're like my brother," Martin replied. "I knew you had to be back soon," said Martin. "And I knew you'd put in a good word for me with your grandfather."

Adam wove his fingers together behind his head and pressed back into his hands in frustration. That was a touching thing for Martin to say, but Adam knew his friend could lay it on thick when he wanted to, and he knew how to say things to *mostly* keep himself out of trouble.

"I think of you like a brother too," said Adam. "But if it was so important to you to do this, and to do it fast, then it was a terrible idea for you to wait for me to help you, because there's nothing I can do! Emmanuel, of all people, is going to think you should have a church wedding, so trying to circumvent the reading of the banns with an expensive marriage bond is not going to be an idea he supports. Your cousin Will is in town, though, so maybe you can go talk him into doing it before he leaves to go back up north."

Martin slapped his knee, then pointed at Adam. "You're right! You're absolutely right! Is he out at the estate right now?"

"Well, he was at the warehouse when I left, but then he was going back to the estate. I reckon if you wait an hour or so, he should be there."

"Good!" Martin said. "I need to handle a couple of things before I go over there, but then I'll go out and talk to him. You wanna hang around and come with me?"

Adam shook his head. "No, thanks. I think maybe this is a conversation y'all ought to have in private, man-to-man. I'll be back at the warehouse, though. We can get some supper at the tavern later if you're up for it."

"Alright. I'll stop back by when I get back into town from my cousin's place."

Adam bade him farewell and returned to the warehouse. As he rode Rex back, he thought about how things might go for Martin if he asked Will to be his bondsman. In truth, he doubted even Will would go along with Martin's idea, but then again, if someone had asked him a month ago if Martin would be burning up to get married, he would've doubted that too.

Chapter Three

WHEN ADAM LEFT MARTIN'S HOUSE, he went back to the warehouse to rest a while. As it turned out, Will had already returned to his sister's house. His grandfather was sitting in his favorite chair reading in his well-worn Bible and scribbling down notes in a little journal.

"Back from Martin's already?" Emmanuel asked, glancing up over the rims of his spectacles.

"Yes, sir," said Adam. He came around and sat on the settee nearest his grandfather.

The old man had a blanket over his legs, which reminded Adam that his grandfather suffered from arthritis. The old man's bones ached as the weather grew colder, and while it was nowhere near freezing, there was a definite chill in the air. Usually by late winter his grandfather would spend a good bit of time under his covers in his bed.

"Did you learn anything new?" Emmanuel asked. It might've seemed strange that Emmanuel would need to ask his grandson, who'd been gone for a month, what one of his own workers was up to lately, but Adam knew Martin was closer to him than anyone else at Rogers's Shipping Company, and that other than Ricky Jones, Martin was unlikely to confide in anyone else who worked there. Even if he *had* confided in Jones, though, he wasn't the sort who'd pass gossip along to others in the company, so Emmanuel didn't know much about Martin's personal life at the moment.

"It's a good thing you're sitting," said Adam. "You'll never believe it when I tell you."

His grandfather placed his ribbon bookmark into his Bible and closed it. He put it and the journal in which he'd been writing on the end table next to his chair. "Well, what is it? Is everything alright?"

"Martin Smith just told me that he and Jenny Green want to get married, and they want to do it right away."

Emmanuel's jaw dropped. "You're joking!" He was evidently as shocked as Adam had been.

"It's true," Adam continued. "And now he knows his cousins are in town, he's gone over to Laney's house to ask Will to be his bondsman."

His grandfather had a sly smile and nodded slowly. "The rascal's finally going to do it then, eh?"

Adam nodded.

"Well, that's just extraordinary," the old man said. "I think this is wonderful news. It's certainly time he settles down, puts down some roots, quits all that whoring around."

"Hard to believe he's ready to give up the bachelor's life, though," said Adam.

Emmanuel nodded. "Indeed, but I say if he's gone so far as to talk to Jenny Green about it, he must be serious."

"Oh, he's serious alright."

"Why on earth doesn't he just have Reverend Miller marry them the normal way?"

"I don't know," Adam said with a shrug. "He acts like his pants are on fire to get married just as fast has he can."

"Hmm." Emmanuel looked pensive. "Well, he better get on with it, then. Else the pair might fall into sin."

Adam chuckled. "I actually think *this* is Martin's way of *escaping* it."

His grandfather smiled and nodded. "I suppose you're right. Well, do tell him if his cousin can't or won't serve as his bondsman for some reason—I know Will is anxious to get on the first ship that's headed north, and the *Gypsy* is leaving again in just a few days—I will put in a good word for him with Reverend Miller, not that that'll help much if anyone has any objections to their union."

"What if for some reason he had to be married by Peter Robins?"

Emmanuel gave him a puzzled look. "The magistrate? Martin's a member at the church and in fair standing, as far as I know. I can't see why he would *have* to get married in a civil service when he can do it the right way, at the church."

Adam shrugged. "Oh, I'm sure he'd like to, but if for some reason Reverend Miller *can't* do it or *won't* do it before the end of the year, would you still be willing to help?"

His grandfather sighed. "Yes, I suppose I would. I reckon if Martin Smith is in a hurry to get married, he probably has a good reason."

"You're probably right." Adam nodded. He stood and said, "I know it's early in the day, but I feel dead on my feet. I think I'd just like to go rest for a little while."

"You do that. Rest is good for you. You want me to wake you up in a couple of hours? Or should I just leave you to sleep."

"Hmm… Martin said he'd come by later, but if he's not

here by six, then yes, please wake me up. I want to go to the tavern this evening to see Mama."

Emmanuel nodded.

Adam went through the little kitchen and through Boaz's room and into his own room at the very back of the living quarters. He hung his coat on a hook on his door and sat on the edge of his bed. He took off his boots, waistcoat, and belt, and adjusted his pillows so he could lean back against them. He really was sleepy, but first, he decided he'd take out his journal and jot a few things down. For the entire return trip, Adam had so many things that he wanted to write about, to remember. He had his new notebook on the trip, but with so many traveling companions on the return journey, he didn't have an opportunity to really spend much time in thought.

And now, as it turned out, nothing came to him. His mind was a blank. He was just too tired.

He put his journal down beside him on the bed and looked out the window. As he gazed out on Taylor Creek, he was suddenly reminded of his father. He remembered how strange it had been to see his father's sloop, *La Dama*, moored at the Rogers's Shipping Company dock almost two months ago. He wondered when he would be coming back to Beaufort, or *if* he would be coming back. It had been weeks now since Santiago had dropped him and the others off in Edenton and headed back to Cuba with half the crew he had started with, thanks to some of the men deciding to become mutineers.

When he thought about his father returning, he felt a pain in his gut and a sense of trepidation. It was unsettling. Adam wasn't sure he even wanted his father to come back. While they had been away, he realized how different they were. Life was far less complicated before they got to know each other. And the fact that his mother seemed less than joyful to have her long-estranged husband back in her life had not escaped him.

He wondered if it was wrong that he felt the way he did. What would happen if his father *did* return to Beaufort? Adam thought that maybe he would just tell him to go on back to Cuba, but he felt guilty about it. After all, it wasn't like Havana was just down the road a little ways. It would be a major expense to even make the trip. A part of him wanted to talk to his grandfather about it, but then another part of him thought he knew what the old man would say. After all, Santiago was his son.

What a mess. Adam decided to put it out of his mind. He lay down and tried to go to sleep.

Apparently, he was successful. A few hours later someone was shaking him by the foot to wake him up.

"Get on up outta bed," said Martin. "Let's go get some supper."

Adam turned over and groaned. He was still tired.

"You keep sleepin, you won't be able to go to sleep later, and that'll mess you up for tomorrow," Martin chided.

Adam grabbed his pocket watch from his dresser and squinted as he tried to make out the time. It was a little after six.

"Fine," he said. He sat up and threw his feet over the side of his bed, then proceeded to put back on his boots, belt, and waistcoat. He grabbed his coat and took a look in the small framed mirror next to his door so he could rearrange the tie that held back his shoulder-length, wavy dark hair. "I look like hell," he said.

"What difference does it make?" Martin said. "We're going to the tavern. It ain't like Laney'll be there."

Adam rolled his eyes. "Let's go, then."

Chapter Four

IT FELT GOOD TO BE back at the Topsail Tavern. While there was a chill outdoors, the tavern was cozy and warm thanks to a crackling fire in the dining room.

Adam had stopped by as soon as he got back into town earlier in the day, but his mother was off visiting with the widow Mitchell and wasn't expected back until evening. For a few years, his mother had taken food to another elderly woman, the widow Simpson, but she passed away about a year ago. In the last few months, she had started looking in on another elderly widow, Mrs. Mitchell. From what he understood, she would take over food and then sit and visit for a few hours. The widow Mitchell had no children, so Mary felt sorry for her that she had no one to care for her.

At this hour, though, Mary was back in the tavern, and she beamed when she saw her son come through the door.

"Valentine told me you had been here!" Mary exclaimed, crossing the dining room to embrace her son. "I'm so relieved to see you! Are you here alone?"

Adam grinned at his mother and then turned to motion to the person standing behind him. "Well, Martin is here."

Mary laughed. "Of course. How are you, Martin?"

Martin grinned and bowed his head. "Fine. Just fine,

thank you, ma'am." He patted Adam on the shoulder and said, "I'm gonna go on and get that table over there."

Adam nodded. "I'll be over in just a little bit." Mary was serving tables, so he knew she wouldn't have long to talk. Their visit would have to wait until after the Topsail closed for the evening. Still, he wanted to speak to her alone for a couple of minutes.

"I'm here alone, Mama. My father had to take some of his men back to Havana. I'm not sure when he'll be back, or if he'll be back."

Mary took a deep breath and let it out quickly, then smiled. "That's alright. I just thank God you're back. I got the letter about you going north, of course, but I didn't know what to expect... when you'd be home... anything." She stepped back and held his hands out to the sides and studied him up and down. "Have you grown?!"

"Ha ha!" Adam was amused. "I didn't think so, but do I look like I have?"

"Maybe a little bit," she said. She gently grabbed his chin and moved his face a bit from side to side. "I think this adventure has aged you some, though. You look older."

Adam shrugged and gave her a grin. "Well, probably I just need some sleep." In truth, he wondered if he *was* "aged" by the trip. It had been a trying journey, physically *and* mentally. It occurred to him that his mother had barely seemed to age in all of his almost twenty years. Her hair was the same color it had always been—dark brown, just like his—and her brown eyes still looked bright. No wrinkles yet, but he did remember she *looked* like she had aged after he came back from Havana the previous year. She had told him that he had aged her ten years while he was gone on that trip.

Just then a gruff sailor sitting with a few other men called out from across the tavern, "Hey, missy! We need another round of drinks over here!"

Mary held up her finger to motion, *Just a minute.*

Adam looked at the man and made an annoyed face. He turned his attention back to his mother. "I'm sorry I worried you. I can tell you all about everything later tonight if you'll be up."

Mary nodded. "I'll be up." She squeezed his arm, then went to tend to the thirsty sailors. "I'll be over to yours and Martin's table in a minute."

Adam gave a nod and he went to join his friend at a table near the fireplace.

"Will won't do it," Martin said without missing a beat.

"What? He won't? What did he say?"

"He said something like what you said, but he just said it a little differently, and that if I'm gonna be married, I need to start actin like a grown man and takin responsibility for my actions." Martin looked annoyed.

"I'm sorry for you," said Adam. "But it'll work out somehow. You just might have to have some patience."

Martin blew air out sharply over his teeth and leaned back in his seat. "I reckon."

"You never did tell me: Why is it you're in such a hurry to get this done? I mean, it's not like you're going off to war or anything."

"I just think it's time," said Martin. "I think—"

Mary came to their table to ask what they wanted for supper.

"What has Aunt Franny made tonight?" said Adam.

"Chicken and pastry or beef stew."

"Beef stew," said Adam.

"I'll have the same," said Martin.

"And what do you boys want to drink?" Mary asked.

"Rum and cider," said Adam.

"Sounds good. I'll have the same," said Martin.

Mary nodded and went to fix their drinks.

"What in the world?" said an amused Adam.

"What?" said Martin.

"You never order exactly what I'm ordering. What's gotten into you?"

"What? Can I help it if you happen to order the same thing I feel like having? Should I be orderin something else just to be contrary?"

Adam wrinkled his brow. "No, but... Well, it's just not like you."

Martin shook his head, but he didn't say anything.

"Anyway, you were telling me," said Adam. "Why are you in such a hurry to get married?"

"Maybe I just don't want somebody else to come along and snap up Jenny. That's what happened last time."

Adam twisted up his face in disbelief. "No, it isn't. That's not what you told me. You always said that you just weren't ready to settle down, and finally Jenny got tired of waiting on you so she married Hardy Greene."

"Same thing," said Martin.

"No, it isn't."

"Jenny is a young, beautiful woman. Don't you reckon if she just sits around and stays single for a while, folks might get to talkin? Like maybe it's indecent or something?"

"What are you talking about?" Adam asked. "Hardy's

only been in the ground a little over a month now. I hardly think that's going to set the tongues to wagging."

Martin leaned forward and pressed his palms against the edge of the table. "Damnit, Fletcher! And what if she were havin a baby?" he whispered forcefully.

Adam's eyes grew wide. "Oh!"

Martin leaned back again and said nothing. He made no effort to hide his frustration with Adam for pressing the matter, though.

"Wait," said Adam. "Is it yours?"

Martin looked across the floor of the dining room, but he still said nothing. Adam could see him swallow hard.

"You don't even know, do you?"

"Maybe it is, maybe it isn't!" Martin snapped. "Does it really make any difference now? I think it's mine, but I don't reckon we'll know until we see it."

Gracious, thought Adam. *That is a big question.* But considering the baby may have been conceived before Hardy died, and Martin and Jenny weren't married yet, it was just as well that they at least acted as though the baby was Hardy's if it turned out they couldn't get married right away. They could hardly admit to the fact that they were with each other before Hardy went to meet his Maker.

Adam knew his friend was in a terrible situation. The only thing he could think of to say was, "Well, it's good that at least you want to make sure the baby has a father to look after it whether it's really yours or not."

Martin sighed, then gave a quick nod.

Just then Mary returned with their drinks.

There was silence between them for a little while until their food was brought to their table. Once they started eating, Adam decided to lighten the mood by talking about his recent adventures.

"Did I tell you we had an attempted mutiny on my father's ship? And a violent storm? And did I mention I was arrested and spent the night in the gaol in Edenton?"

Martin's jaw dropped. "No, I reckon I'd remember it if you had!"

Adam proceeded to fill Martin in on the details that he'd left out when he had spoken to him earlier in the day. It provided a welcome transition away from the weightier topic of Martin and Jenny's current situation. He didn't mention getting lashed, though. He didn't want his mother to find out, and keeping it to himself was the best way to do that, he thought.

Once they were done eating, Martin told Adam it was good to have him back in town and that he reckoned he would just see him at work the next day. Adam bade him farewell and then went over to the bar, until it was time for the tavern to close for the evening.

He talked to Valentine while his mother took care of the last couple of tables of diners.

"It's a good thing you're back," said Valentine with a grin. "I was starting to wonder if I was going to have to go hunt down the greenery all by myself."

"Gracious," Adam said in surprise. "Is it already that time?"

"Advent is Sunday after next, and you know that's always when we hang the greens around here. The patrons like it." Valentine smiled proudly.

"Well, I'll be ready whenever you are," Adam responded.

The older Adam got and the more time he spent around

his devout, church-attending grandfather, the more he noticed the little inconsistencies he'd grown up around at the tavern. He could probably count on two hands the number of times he'd been in the local church with Valentine *or* his mother, and yet they still thought of themselves as Christians, and they observed all the regular holidays, like Advent, even if it was in unorthodox ways. One of these days he would have to ask either his mother or Valentine why they did things the way they did.

Today marked the midpoint of November—the fifteenth—and indeed Christmas was now less than six weeks away. It had always been a tradition that the Topsail Tavern had special greenery up to mark the season, from Advent Sunday through the Epiphany on January 6.

There would be little wreaths of evergreen in every window and a whole bough of it on the mantel with an Advent wreath as its centerpiece, a new "candle" being lit for each Sunday of Advent, except they used small lanterns instead of actual candles, since they kept them burning all day throughout Advent season. The most memorable decoration for Adam was always the cluster of mistletoe that hung from the ceiling just inside the tavern's entrance. When he was little, he would go with Valentine to the woods just north of town to hunt all of their greenery and for the perfect bunch of mistletoe at the top of a tall tree. Sure, they might find some on lower boughs closer to the tavern, but for Adam, hunting for that perfect cluster was always part of the fun—and he remembered it as something that marked the transition from him being a little boy to being a young man.

When Adam was very small, Valentine would climb up a tree to gather the elusive bundle of greenery and berries. He wouldn't let Adam scale the tree himself, though—not until he was almost ten years old. He'd never forget the Christmas just before the March when he turned ten. That was the year Valentine finally said he was big enough to climb up that tall tree all by himself. From that day forward, he would play a valuable role in helping the Topsail Tavern usher in the Christmas season. In fact, on that day, at the ripe old age of nine and three-quarters, he knew the responsibility had passed to him, and he felt like he had become a man.

One thing he missed at Rogers's Shipping Company was decorating for Christmas. It wasn't that Emmanuel was opposed to Christmas decorations, but he didn't much see the point of having them. Boaz certainly wouldn't be the one to take the initiative to bring in festive greenery. And Adam understood why there would be no mistletoe. In the entire time he had been an apprentice at the warehouse, he had never known a member of the fairer sex to come up to the living quarters. There would be no need for mistletoe with just a bunch of men around.

Admittedly, Valentine always said having the decorations was good for business—they put people in a good mood around Christmastime—and the sailors loved that mistletoe, especially on those occasions when they would bring a female companion.

Adam remembered Valentine's late wife, Margaret, telling him about the Christmas traditions where she came from. Her family were Palatine immigrants who had come to the colony as part of the mostly Swiss settlement of 1710. She would often talk about Christmas in Germany, even though she was a little girl when they came to America. The strangest thing to Adam was the idea of having a whole *tree* decorated with cookies and candles and who knows what else? He never was clear on whether it was some kind of tree grown for the purpose, or if they had just gone into the woods and cut one down, and he never thought to press her for an answer when she was still living.

Soon, the last patrons left the establishment, and Valentine slipped out back through the kitchen to return to his cottage, leaving Adam and his mother to visit in the empty tavern. Adam helped his mother lock up for the night.

"You want me to fix you a cup of tea? Or maybe flip?" Mary asked her son.

Adam nodded. "Tea would be good, I think. Thank you."

Mary went into the kitchen, with Adam following close behind. As he gave her a short summary of his recent travels, she took the kettle off of the fire, and then she took two mugs from a nearby sideboard and drizzled some honey in the bottom of each before pouring hot water over strainers of tea leaves into each of them.

Adam went over to a cupboard where he knew Aunt Franny often kept leftover sweets and pastries, and he was happy to find some molasses cake. There wasn't much left, so he took what was there and sat down in one of the chairs near the long table where food preparation was normally done and waited for his mother to join him.

Once they were both sitting down to have tea and cake, Mary said, "I'm just thankful you're back. You're going to kill me with worry. Do you know that?"

Adam smiled. "I'm sorry, Mama, but you shouldn't worry so much. I'm grown now. Sometimes I'm going to have to go places, take care of things. Doesn't mean I'm doing anything dangerous." He felt a pang of guilt as he said it. He knew most of his adventures outside of Beaufort led him directly into some kind of danger.

Mary broke off a corner from the molasses cake and popped it in her mouth. She studied her son's face and said, "Why do I get the sneaking suspicion there's something you're not telling me?"

Adam lifted his mug to take a sip, but he burnt his lip. He shook his head. "I don't know. Because you like to worry, I guess."

He felt even more guilty now. There was *a lot* he wasn't telling her, but he didn't see how letting her know about *everything* that had happened on his trip would be helpful. It would probably only serve to make her even more of a nervous wreck the next time he left town.

"Your father's gone back to Havana, then?"

Adam nodded. "Are you mad? Or are you relieved?"

Mary tipped her head to the side and gave a half smile. "A little bit of both, I guess. Things feel more back to normal."

"I understand. You know, he's not really like I thought he'd be. Not that I ever knew, really, what to expect, but he's just so different than... well, different than all of us. He didn't really want to get involved with helping Charles Jr., you know. I think he would've been just fine if we went on back to Beaufort and that would've been it."

"What would you expect?" Mary shrugged. "He grew up in a different place with a *very* different upbringing. And his family was *rich*. Very rich. I reckon that had something to do with the way he looked at the world. I reckon his family has always had a lot of slaves, and I also would think, given the circumstances of having that sugar plantation, they didn't have the same kinds of relationships with them as we would with, say, Aunt Franny, or the way the Martins are over Aunt Celie and their other help. I think things are different when we're doing work alongside the help than when folks are sitting up in their fancy houses while the help does all the work out in distant fields."

"Eh, maybe." Adam lifted his mug to his lips to see if the tea had cooled enough to sip. It had. He needed to stir in the honey a little bit more, though. "But really, do you think Laney Martin has ever had to lift a finger to work alongside her family's slaves?"

Mary shook her head. "No, probably not, but in her family's case, Aunt Celie and Old Charles helped raise up her and Will. And the two of them had been with Laney's mother and father when they were growing up, too, so it's different. I don't think that's something your father understands or has any experience with."

Adam shrugged. "I guess."

"Listen, I'm thirty-seven years old now. It was more than twenty years ago when I met your father. I was practically a child. Knowing what I know now, if I met him, I don't think I'd have been drawn to him like I was then. When I was a girl, he was just so exotic, exciting"—she waved her hands around—"and he was surely better looking than most of the old salts who wander into this place." She laughed. "You're even more handsome than he was, you know. But that's because you've got my blood too."

Adam grinned sheepishly. "Well, I reckon it's a good thing I'm tied up with my apprenticeship for another year and almost four months, right? So that way I can't just rush off and get married to someone who might not be the best choice."

Mary looked pensive as she pressed her lips together and narrowed her eyes. "Hmm… I get the feeling you've already grown quite a bit in these last couple of years. You'd probably make a better choice than I did then. You were about my age when you busted Francis Smythe in the nose just outside this tavern. I don't reckon you'd pull a stunt like that now, would you?"

"I don't know," said Adam. "If he came in here running his mouth like he was that day, I may… I don't know that I'd change anything about that fight, though. If it hadn't happened, I'd have never gone to stay with Emmanuel, and I'd have never learned about who my father was, or Emmanuel. That's changed a lot for me. At least people aren't talking about us like they used to anymore."

"Maybe they aren't. Maybe they are. How would you even know? And more importantly, why would you care?"

"You always used to say that. 'Why would you care?' I'm your son, and I'm a man. I would be a failure at both if I just sat by and let people disparage your name. At least I reckon I've become a little bit more tempered if someone says something about *me*."

"Well, let's talk about something more important," Mary said, resting her hands on her knees. "How are things with you and Laney Martin?"

Adam had been taking a sip of tea and he nearly choked. His mother's question had come so out of the blue.

"What do you mean, how are things with me and Laney Martin?"

"It sounds like y'all went through quite an adventure together recently. Did y'all have much time to talk?"

Adam chuckled. It was awkward to talk about Laney,

especially with his mother. "To be honest, not much time. We stayed in completely different parts of *La Dama* on the trip back to North Carolina, and otherwise, we were always with her brother or Aunt Celie or somebody. But what would you expect us to talk about?"

Mary shrugged and gave a sneaky smile. "I don't know... I'm just wondering if there might be some interest between you. Well, I know there must be some, but I'm just wondering if either of you have had the nerve to talk about it yet."

Adam could feel his cheeks getting warm. He hoped his mother couldn't see his color change. The last thing he needed right now was someone else telling him he should have a talk with Laney about the future.

"Mama, if there's ever anything for you to know, believe me, I'll tell you. But on the subject of women, did you know that Martin Smith is finally going to settle down?" He was pleased with his ability to deflect her questions.

Mary's eyes became like saucers. "Do what?! When? With who?"

"Jenny Greene."

"Jenny Greene? Her husband's only been in the ground a month! She's already getting remarried?"

Adam nodded. "Yep. The two of them want to tie the knot right away. Anyway, maybe you didn't know, but they were sweethearts as kids. I think now that Jenny's been left a widow, Martin has decided to finally grow up and settle down. He wants to look after Jenny."

Mary sighed, and then she smiled. "Well, I suppose that's a good thing." She stood from her chair and took her mug across the kitchen to wash it out in the dishpan before putting it back on the shelf. "I just hope he's serious about it and isn't just making a hasty move because of everything that's happened recently."

"Oh, I think he's serious about it."

He brought his mug over to his mother, and she washed it and put it on the shelf. Mary reached her arms up around his neck and gave him a hug.

"I still think you're getting taller, you know. Seems like I keep having to reach up a little further."

"Maybe so," said Adam. "I figure it's about time for me to stop growing now, though, isn't it?"

"I reckon, but since you're still a growing boy, go on back to the warehouse and get some rest. Will you be back over here tomorrow?"

"Probably. Depends on what Emmanuel has us doing. I reckon I might come by midday, but if not, probably by supper."

He bade his mother goodnight and left through the kitchen door, while she went back through the tavern and upstairs to the old room, where he had spent most of his life. He thought to himself he might like to see that room again sometime soon, just to remember where he grew up.

Chapter Five

THE AIR WAS CHILLY ALONG Taylor Creek as Adam walked back to the warehouse. He thought about his conversations with Martin, and Valentine, and his mother. Seemed there was a lot to look forward to in the coming weeks or months—especially with Martin's pending nuptials and the surprises that might bring.

He also thought about December and going with Valentine to get the evergreens and mistletoe. And mistletoe made him think of kissing. And kissing made him think of Laney Martin. His thoughts drifted to whether or not there might be any chance to get Laney to come by the Topsail Tavern over the Christmas season so perhaps he could sneak a quick peck on the cheek beneath the mistletoe.

And then he was suddenly disgusted with himself. He had *never* been reserved around girls before. He was so confident when he first met Laney, and really, his whole life, but since their recent adventures something had changed. He knew she cared for him. He cared for her. He knew he wanted to marry her one day, but he also thought it was a bad idea to let his thoughts go too far down that road. Laney was a virtuous young woman, and Adam was no Martin Smith and he had no desire become one. After all, he'd been by Martin's side through some of his most humiliating episodes. The fact that Martin had the morals of a stray dog caused him to go through some dark times.

Adam would be twenty in March. Just one more year until he could finish his apprenticeship, but then what? He wasn't independently wealthy. He still didn't have any means to buy land or build a house, and where would he and Laney live if they *did* get married? A room at the tavern? Or his room at the warehouse? Would he be a kept husband and just happily go live in her house without having much yet to contribute to their marriage? Of course not. So again, it made no sense to get worked up thinking about any of that when there was nothing he could do to be a worthy husband. It would all just have to wait.

But still, surely a quick kiss on the cheek under the mistletoe for Christmas could tide him over. He hoped. He consoled himself thinking that since Laney was a girl, she was unlikely to be battling the same thoughts and desires that he was. Surely she would have no problem being patient and waiting until the right time for him to discuss the future with her.

When he got back to the warehouse and went up to the living quarters, he was surprised to find his grandfather and Boaz still awake and playing chess. It was close to midnight, which could only mean they were getting close to ending this game. They would often keep a game going for days at a time. He had noticed the pieces arranged on the board when he came in earlier in the day, but he had no idea how long the match had been going on.

"Y'all are up late," he said as he stood near the table to observe the board.

"I think we'll stop soon," Emmanuel said. "What time is it, anyway?"

"Almost midnight," said Adam.

"I'm done," Boaz said. "Maybe we'll finish this tomorrow," he said to Emmanuel. "And I'll win."

Emmanuel waved his hand dismissively at the gruff, middle-aged cooper. "You always say that, but at least half the time you're wrong."

Adam shook his head in amusement.

Boaz left the room to go to bed. Adam sat down in his seat.

"How was supper?" Emmanuel asked. "I'll bet your mother was happy to see you."

"She was. We had a good visit."

"Anything new from Martin?"

Adam nodded. "Yep. He said Will won't be his bondsman. He's going with Jenny tomorrow to talk to Reverend Miller."

"I think everything will work out fine," Emmanuel said. "I know Martin has lived a roguish life thus far, but I doubt they'll have any serious objections come up to their marriage."

"Serious objections?"

"Well, when the Reverend asks if anyone has any objection, he doesn't just mean a jealous girl from years ago. There would have to be a serious reason. You know how this works."

"True. I've told him the same thing, but I'm not surprised he's worried his past might catch up to him."

Emmanuel folded his hands on the table in front of him. "You've always been a good friend to Martin. He's fortunate to have you."

Adam shrugged. "He was my first and *only* real friend

when I first came here. He kind of took me under his wing. I reckon we're a little bit like brothers."

Emmanuel chuckled. "You know, I suppose it's fitting. Back in our sailing days, his grandfather and I were particularly close as well. Of course that's how he ended up working here, and it's how I ended up using Rocksolanah's estate as my second dock."

"Really? Huh. I reckon I always knew you had been friends with Martin and Laney's grandfather, but I didn't realize you were close."

"Oh, we were thick as thieves, us two. And to tell you the truth, he's not terribly different from his grandfather. They've both been rascals in their day."

Adam grinned in amusement. "So I'm more like you, huh?"

"A good bit you are, yes, but I'll admit I was more reserved than you. You've always been more confident than I was as a lad."

That response surprised Adam. "You were more reserved and I've been more confident? I hardly see how that's possible. You sailed with the most infamous pirate of the century!"

"Eh, it was work. And a sort of camaraderie, but we each had our duties to perform in the crew. You should know that not all pirates are as boisterous as you've read about."

"I remember." Adam smiled. He thought back to the conversation he'd had with Emmanuel shortly after coming to work at the shipping company when he learned his master had once sailed with Blackbeard. He didn't know yet that the old man was his grandfather.

"Well, like you said, it's late. And you have work tomorrow," said Emmanuel.

"True." Adam stood from his chair and pushed it back under the table. "I reckon I better get some sleep then. Goodnight."

"Goodnight."

Monday it was time for Adam to get reacquainted with his routine at the warehouse. For the first time in nearly two months, things were finally starting to feel back to normal.

The *Gypsy* was scheduled to leave for Philadelphia on Thursday. The sloop would be carrying a variety of locally produced items for northern buyers. There were several pallets of cedar shingles, and soon there would be dozens of casks of turpentine and pitch.

At noontime, Martin left to pick up Jenny so they could see Reverend Miller about getting married. If all went according to plan, the first reading of the banns might happen on Sunday.

When he came back to the warehouse, everyone was eager to hear how it went.

"It wasn't as bad as I thought it would be," said Martin. "The good Reverend seemed sort of skeptical at first, but after we talked a little bit, he acted just as enthusiastic as we were for us to tie the knot."

"That's good!" said Adam. He was relieved for his friend's sake that the meeting had gone well.

"Congratulations, mate!" said Ricky Jones. Jones normally sailed on the *Gypsy*, but for the upcoming trip to Philadelphia, he would be staying behind so Joe Salter could sail with the crew. Jones was no master cooper, but he was a hard worker and could help with just about any task.

Joe Salter and his cousin Elliot had worked at Rogers's

Shipping Company since long before Adam was apprenticed there. Elliot was usually talkative, whereas Joe hardly ever said a word. Recently, however, Joe apparently decided he needed some adventure in his own life and he was ready to see the world, so he figured Philadelphia would be a good place to start.

Earlier that day, while Adam was recounting some of his adventures to the other men, he learned that Salter's Ferry, the place where they had found Annabelle's half sister, was named for one of Joe and Elliot's uncles—another Pamlico River family with pirates in their history.

The rest of Monday was uneventful. It was a relief to Adam that everything was finally back to normal.

On Monday morning he had been so tired when he rolled out of bed that he didn't take much time to think about anything except finally getting back to work, but Tuesday morning, Adam was sleeping so soundly in his bed it finally took Emmanuel coming into his room to wake him after Boaz had already tried and failed twice. It wasn't because he was so tired this time, but because he was the most comfortable he'd been since he could remember. He felt overwhelming gratitude when his eyes adjusted to the new day and he could drink in the view from the window beside his bed. It overlooked Taylor Creek, and the way the sun hit it just right first thing in the morning made the water glisten. He didn't realize how much he had missed that.

After breakfast with his grandfather—Boaz had already gone down to the warehouse to start working—Adam energetically bounded down the stairs to get to work.

It was another uneventful day until just after they had taken a break for their midday meal.

Adam, Boaz, Martin, Elliot, and Joe were putting the finishing touches on the last few casks, while Ricky Jones was off delivering a cartful to the Wiggins's place so they could be filled with pitch before Thursday.

Elliot was telling some story about a man he had seen the previous evening at Russell's Tavern, which was on the other side of town from the Topsail. Adam and the others all turned and looked when the bay door on the street side of the warehouse swung open and two figures paused in the doorway.

"Can I help you?" called out Boaz.

The visitors strode menacingly into the building, but then they slowed their pace when the swarthy, curly haired cooper stood, dusted his calloused hands on his work apron, and turned to face them.

Boaz was almost fifty years old, but his muscular frame still cut an imposing figure.

With light streaming in behind them, the two visitors were cloaked in shadow until they came nearer to their work area.

Suddenly, Adam heard Martin swear under his breath. Adam gave a quizzical look to his friend. Martin gave a quick, subtle shake of his head as if to say, *Not now!* With that, Adam suspected he knew who the men were.

"We're here to have a word with Martin Smith," said the older of the two.

Martin didn't make eye contact with them. Instead, he looked at Boaz. Adam saw panic in Martin's eyes.

The visitors were evidently Henry and Bill Greene, the brothers of the late Hardy Greene, and from what Adam had heard, that would mean the older one had to be Henry.

Boaz wrinkled his brow in confusion at Martin, then turned his attention back towards the visitors.

"This is a place of business," said Boaz, "and Smith is busy working. Whatever it is'll have to wait until we finish up for the day. That is, unless you want to say what you need to say right here."

Henry and Bill Greene looked at each other and whispered something, and then Henry said, "That's fine. We can say what we was gonna say right here." The pair took steps towards Martin, until Boaz took steps towards them.

Henry raised up his arm and pointed his finger at Martin. "You son of a bitch, we just got word you're plannin to marry Jenny. Our brother ain't barely even in the ground a month and you think you gon swoop right in and take his widow and his house and all of it?"

Martin looked at them and said, "I plan to look out for Jenny, to take care of her. Surely y'all don't think she should be left alone, do you?"

At that, the younger brother, Bill, bolted towards Martin, until Boaz and Adam came between the two and held Bill off from his target.

Bill continued forcefully shoving his pointed finger forward and said, "I'm gon kick your ass, boy! You killed Hardy! I'm gon kick your ass all the way from here to Ocracoke and then back again!"

Has he lost his mind? Adam wondered. "Hardy Greene's heart stopped and Martin was nowhere near him when it happened. How can you claim he killed your brother?"

Bill's face was beet red and his eyes were watery. Adam could tell he was too upset to even answer. That's when Henry said, "Won't nothin in the world wrong with Hardy's heart!

We been hearin all about how them gypsies that were here were peddlin curses and all kinds of wickedness, and we got a witness who said they saw Martin Smith visit that old gypsy witch! So we know he done it so he can take our brother's wife. And damnit all, we reckon he might've had a curse put on Jenny, too, to make her forget our brother so quick and be willin to marry his sorry tail!"

"You're a damned liar!" Martin countered. "Your brother paid that gypsy woman to try to kill *me*!"

This time, Henry rushed forward, but Elliot and Joe intervened to hold him off.

Henry raised up his hands to let them know he wouldn't push further, but he said to Martin. "Now you're lyin on my brother's memory! I might not can prove that you tried to kill him, but I got witnesses right here, and now you've just lied on my brother, and we ain't gon let you get away with it!"

Adam shook his head. "Look, I don't know y'all, but you've got this all wrong. I was with Martin when he went to see Madame Endora, the old gypsy woman, and he didn't ask her to do anything to your brother. In fact, it *was* your brother who tried to pay *her* to put a curse on *him*. She nearly killed him, too, with that fake medicine she sent him."

Henry and Bill both looked incensed. Bill said, "Now you're lyin on our brother too! We'll give both of y'all a whippin!"

"Enough!" Boaz bellowed in his gruff voice. "Nobody's whippin anybody right now! We've got work to finish."

Just then Emmanuel called from the upstairs balcony, "What's all the commotion down there?"

Boaz responded, "These men have a bone to pick with

Smith, but I've told them it'll have to wait until we're done with work for the day."

The typically spritely old man was a little bit stiff as he made his way down the stairs and to the warehouse floor. He crossed over to where all of the men stood and he asked the Greene brothers, "Who are you? And what sort of problem is this?"

Henry answered, "I'm Henry Greene and this is my brother Bill. We've just heard that sorry Martin Smith is planning to marry the widow of our recently deceased brother, Hardy, and we suspect he might've had somethin to do with his death."

Bill nodded. "That's right, and we can't just let that go by unpunished."

"Good heavens!" Emmanuel exclaimed. "What on earth would make you think Mr. Smith had anything to do with that?"

"The way he done swooped in and convinced Jenny to marry him so quick. It don't seem right!"

Emmanuel grimaced, and he shook his head. "Listen, lads, I understand you're upset about your brother, but you're not thinking rationally. Mr. Smith couldn't have had anything to do with your brother's death. In fact, he had been confined to his own sick bed when he received word of your brother's passing."

Henry and Bill seemed unfazed by Emmanuel's defense.

"That gypsy woman had somethin to do with it," said Bill. "And now he's tryin to turn things around and lie about our dead brother and blame Hardy for tryin to kill *him*."

Adam was amused as he watched his grandfather lower

his head and rub his forehead in frustration. *He thinks these men are idiots. So do I.*

Emmanuel raised his head. "What solution do you propose? Because if either of you try to take matters into your own hands and you attack Mr. Smith, I can assure you that it's highly probable that his own friends"—he motioned to Boaz and Adam and the others—"some of whom you see here, will come after you to seek revenge. And so it will go, on and on and on."

The brothers both took deep breaths and sighed in frustration almost in unison.

"We already done said that we have a witness that he went to see that old gypsy woman, and we think he hired her to curse our brother. We're gon take that witness to the constable and make a complaint about this. And another thing: you can be sure that we'll be at the church house on Sunday to object when the Reverend reads the banns."

"What fools!" Emmanuel exclaimed. "Are you lads still so caught up in old superstitions that you honestly think a woman has the power to simply put a curse on a man and kill him? How absurd!"

"Say what you want, old man!" said Bill. "Whether or not she *could* do it ain't really the point, is it? If *he* thought she could and then he hired her to do it, well, I reckon that's attempted murder, ain't it?"

Emmanuel shook his head in disbelief. He waved his hands at all of them dismissively and crossed the warehouse and climbed the stairs. Once he got up to the balcony, he called down, "Put an end to this nonsense and get back to work." He opened and shut the door to the upstairs living quarters forcefully.

Adam and the others, aside from the Greene brothers, looked at each other with raised eyebrows and surprised faces. Emmanuel *rarely* lost his temper, but he seemed to have been awfully close just then.

"Does Jenny know y'all came here?" Martin asked Henry and Bill.

"We don't need to check in with her," said Henry. "She may know or maybe she don't, but it makes no difference. It's as simple as this: you ain't gon marry Jenny. And don't be surprised if the constable don't come and haul you off to the gaol sooner than you think. And if that don't do the trick, we'll make sure the Reverend won't marry you. We have a valid objection."

"We've got work to do. You boys need to get on out of here," said Boaz, "or the only thing the constable will be coming here for is to investigate an assault, 'cause I'll kick both of your asses myself."

Henry and Bill exchanged a blank look and then they left the warehouse, speaking in hushed voices as they walked out. They turned back and looked in Martin's direction once more and laughed hard and loud before leaving the building altogether.

Adam was glad they were gone. He figured he understood what their strategy was now, and they weren't as stupid as they looked. The Greene brothers' chief goal was to destroy Martin's life and his chances of a joyful future with their brother's widow. It made no difference to them whether Martin was actually guilty of any crime. He guessed they were offended that Jenny was moving on so quickly after their brother's death, and that Martin was her coconspirator in this happiness scheme. He also suspected that the Greene brothers might have known something, or heard something, about Martin and Jenny's ongoing affair. Finally, he couldn't help but wonder if the property that had belonged to the late Hardy, but that would now fall into Martin's possession, was a motivator in their determination to put a stop to Martin and Jenny's marriage. Since Jenny hadn't given Hardy any heirs, they likely hated the thought of Greene property going into Martin's hands. And it was unlikely they'd be comforted knowing that Jenny was with child, given the question about the paternity.

In truth, Adam couldn't say he blamed them for their frustration, but still, their attempts to ruin Martin and Jenny's life together could only yield a pyrrhic victory.

BY LATE AFTERNOON, ONLY BOAZ, Adam, and Martin were left in the warehouse.

"You fellas want to come to the Topsail for supper?" Adam asked as he finished moving the last of the casks they had been working on that day over near the bay doors so they could be delivered and filled with pitch the next morning.

Boaz wrinkled his brow. He was likely surprised by Adam's invitation. Adam had never invited him to have a meal at the tavern before. He stretched his back before removing his work apron and hanging it on one of the hooks near their work area.

"Ah no, thanks," he said. "Elliot invited me to eat at his house tonight. His wife's made some kind of thing from Sweden, and he wanted me to try it." He made a nervous but funny expression.

"I reckon that'll be interesting," said Martin. "Wonder how it'll be."

"Yeah," said Adam. "I'm actually kind of curious. You'll have to let us know how it is."

Elliot and his wife, Ana, had been married less than a year. Adam had heard that she and her family had moved to the colony when she was only about twelve years old, and they moved to Beaufort just before she turned twenty—close to the same time Adam started working at the warehouse. Elliot had talked many times before he started courting her about how much he liked her accent. He would say, "Woo! The way she talks makes me right weak in the knees!"

Adam and Martin always laughed when he did. One thing the men at the warehouse would laugh about was that Ana was kind of a big girl—pretty, though—while Elliot was skinny as a rail. They would joke with him and say she looked like she could pick him up and carry him across the threshold when they got married. Elliot didn't mind, though. He would always just respond with, "That just means there's more of her for me to love on!"

Martin still hadn't responded to Adam's supper invitation.

"Martin? You want to come over to the Topsail to eat?"

Martin shook his head. "Can't do it. Jenny's fixin supper for us at her house. I'll be over there."

Boaz said he wanted to go clean up before he went to Elliot's house, so he excused himself to go upstairs to the living quarters.

Adam was left sweeping the warehouse floor, and Martin was just about to leave when he walked over to him and said, "You know, I hope those Greene boys don't mess up everything with Jenny."

Adam stopped sweeping. He stood with the broom

propped in his hand and stared at the floor, unsure of what to say.

"I know. I hate it for you," he said. He looked up at Martin and shook his head. "I don't know what to tell you other than you might want to go ahead and talk to the Reverend about it before those boys have a chance to poison the well, so to speak."

Martin sighed. "Yeah. You're prob'ly right."

Adam started sweeping again as he continued their conversation. "I think it'll be alright. Reverend Miller is a good man. He's fair, and I think if you explain things to him truthfully, he'll be able to give you some good advice about the situation."

Martin nodded, but he didn't say anything at first. He started to walk towards the bay doors to leave the warehouse, then turned around and said, "How 'bout you go over there with me in the morning?"

Adam looked up from his sweeping. "You don't think you should just handle this yourself?"

"I prob'ly should, but I'm afraid I might not go through with it if it's just up to me."

Adam understood what he meant. What Martin really wanted was for Adam to make sure he *did* go and talk to the Reverend, and that he said the right things.

"Alright," he said. "I'll go."

They agreed Adam would meet Martin at his house at seven o'clock in the morning and they'd go right from there to the rectory.

Chapter Six

FIRST THING WEDNESDAY MORNING, ADAM and Martin did just as they had planned. Adam showed up at seven, and they went to go talk to Reverend Miller about the Greene brothers, and to seek advice about how Martin should handle it. Adam had made up his mind he wouldn't say anything unless it became apparent he should.

Martin knocked on the door of the rectory. It took a moment, but finally a short, stout woman who looked like she was probably in her late fifties answered the door.

"May I help you?" she said.

Martin looked at Adam, then said to her, "Ma'am, I'm Martin Smith. I need to speak with the Reverend Miller. Is he in?"

The woman nodded. "One moment please."

She left them standing on the porch.

A few seconds later Reverend Miller came to the door. "Come in, lads. Come have a seat here in the parlor."

The middle-aged Reverend Miller was tall and of average weight, and his hair was sparse. He typically looked serious, but his kindness would come through in conversation. He showed Adam and Martin to a sunny room right near the front door and motioned for them to sit wherever they liked.

Once they were all seated—Martin and Adam in two short-backed, dark-green chairs by the window, Reverend Miller in a similar, burgundy-colored chair nearby—the Reverend said, "What brings you lads here today?"

Martin looked at Adam in slight panic before responding. Adam just gave him a nod of encouragement, as if to say, *Go ahead.* They had talked about what he would say while they were on their way over, but the situation did feel a bit more nerve-racking than they had imagined it would be.

"Well, Reverend, as I'm sure you recall, I was in here on Monday with Jenny Greene because we want to get married, and you said that you'd publish the banns for the first time this Sunday."

Reverend Miller nodded. "Indeed, I do remember."

Martin clasped his hands and smiled nervously. "We are so grateful to you for that, sir." He evidently was waiting for the Reverend to respond, but he didn't, so Martin continued. "Well, the reason I'm here today, ah… You see, yesterday at the warehouse we had some unexpected visitors show up, and I think they're not too happy about me and Jenny."

"Oh?" The Reverend looked puzzled.

Adam wished Martin would just get on with it. He was making himself seem more suspicious the longer he stammered trying to get out what he wanted to say. He noticed the Reverend seemed confounded as well.

Finally, Martin said, "Hardy's brothers came to the warehouse yesterday and made a ridiculous claim that I can *prove* is a lie, and I think the only reason they're sayin it is because they don't want me and Jenny to get married."

Reverend Miller raised his eyebrows and took a deep breath through his nostrils as he appeared to consider what

Martin had said. He even glanced in Adam's direction, probably wondering if he might have something to add. He didn't.

"Martin, on one hand, surely we can understand that they might be a *wee bit* bothered that their sister-in-law is moving on so quickly after their brother's death, but in my experience it's not uncommon for a young widow to quickly remarry." He glanced off to the side and added, almost under his breath, "Of course those widows *do* typically have young children." He redirected his attention to Martin. "Nevertheless, if as you say their claim is demonstrably false, I don't think you have anything to be concerned about. The two of you clearly love each other deeply."

Martin nodded. "Oh, we do, sir. We sure definitely do!"

"What accusation have the Greene brothers made?"

Martin looked at Adam, possibly for some encouragement, before answering, "They claim I tried to get that old gypsy woman that was here about six weeks ago to put a hex on their brother, and that that's what killed him. They said they're going to object to the wedding *and* take their complaint to the constable and say I attempted murder."

"Oh I see," was all that Reverend Miller said.

"And it's just ridiculous, because all I wanted was to get my fortune read. It was actually Hardy Greene who went to the old gypsy to put a curse on *me*! Can you believe this?"

What a stupid thing to say! Adam was dumbfounded that Martin added that unnecessary last bit of information.

Reverend Miller rubbed his forehead with his fingers and then sighed. He clasped his hands together in his lap. "You must know I would be remiss if I didn't tell you that I'm disappointed to hear you went to the gypsy camp. I even preached on the subject."

Martin nodded. "I know, sir, and I'm sorry. Believe me, I know better now."

"Well, the good news is that I know God is sovereign, whereas gypsy curses are wholly impotent. The only real danger that can come to someone relevant to gypsy 'curses' is the spiritual harm that follows disobedience to God. And whether you *or* Hardy Greene tried to solicit the gypsy woman to tell a fortune or put a curse on anyone, you are *both* guilty of giving the devil an invitation to meddle in your lives by going to a seer."

Adam desperately wanted to mention how Martin nearly died because of the gypsy woman's concoction, so he might've already paid the price for that particular sin, but he thought better of it.

"So, are you saying I don't need to worry about any of this as it relates to my marriage to Jenny?" Martin asked.

"I didn't say that. If the Greene brothers voice their objection before the congregation, I have no choice but to hear them out. After all, that's why the banns are read. And even if they take their claim to the constable and it goes to the magistrate, I doubt Mr. Robins would entertain the notion of attempted murder by means of a gypsy's curse, but he might be interested in knowing whether or not anyone has proof of the claim that you solicited the woman for a curse to kill Hardy Greene. If they had some witness to their claim, you might well find yourself being reprimanded for the intent."

"But I didn't do it! I went to her to have my fortune read! That was it! The old gypsy could verify that herself."

Adam nodded. "That's true, and if she were here, she could also tell how Hardy Greene actually went to her to have a curse put on Martin. She told me that herself."

The Reverend shook his head in disbelief. There was an awkward silence for a moment, and then he said, "For my part, I'm afraid that unless and until the Greene brothers bring forth their objection once the banns are read, there's nothing that can be done just yet." He looked solemnly at Martin. "I suggest you spend some sincere time in prayer and reflection. It sounds to me like there is enmity between you and the Greenes that existed before Hardy's death. I'm not exactly sure what that's about, and I'm not going to ask, but I will tell you that nothing you do is hidden from God, but perhaps more importantly, there is no sin so great that the blood of Jesus Christ cannot cover it. Thanks to our Lord's abundant mercy, you can be as pure as snow in His eyes."

Martin looked down as if he had been punched in the gut. Then he took a deep breath and nodded. "Yes, sir."

The Reverend stood from his chair and held out his hands as though he was about to show Martin and Adam out of the parlor.

Martin and Adam stood. The Reverend shook Martin's hand and then Adam's and bade them farewell.

WHEN THEY LEFT THE RECTORY, Adam and Martin went straight to the warehouse to help out with whatever last-minute things were needed before the *Gypsy's* departure tomorrow. When the workday was done, it occurred to Adam he should go out to Laney's house to see Will before he left the next morning.

His grandfather gave him permission to take Rex, so he rode out to Lennoxville Point for the first time since they had all arrived back in Beaufort on Sunday.

He tied Rex up to the hitching post by the back porch, and then he went up to the door and pulled the cord that rang the bell. When Annabelle answered, he was caught off-guard for a split second. He wasn't used to seeing her *or* Charles Jr. in Beaufort.

Annabelle showed him in and offered to take his coat to hang on the wall hook.

"You doing alright, Miss Annabelle?" he asked.

"Yes sir, I sure am. Who are you wantin to see, so I can let 'em know you're here?"

"I came to see Will before he leaves tomorrow."

Annabelle nodded. "Come on in and have a seat in the parlor. He'll be right with you."

While Adam waited for Will, he wondered what Laney was doing, or if he should've told Annabelle he was there to see Will *and* Laney.

It made little difference. Soon Will came through the foyer and into the parlor.

Adam stood to shake his hand.

"Fletcher, good to see you."

Will motioned for Adam to have a seat on the settee, and he sat in an elegantly upholstered chair nearby—both were much fancier than the furniture in the rectory.

"I was just upstairs making sure I've got everything in order for tomorrow."

"That's good to hear. I was just wondering if you're looking forward to the trip, or if you've figured out yet what you'll do for that leg between Philadelphia and Boston."

"I actually visited with Captain Carl Phillips yesterday. He said there's a packet ship that goes between Philadelphia and Boston weekly. I shouldn't have any problem getting passage on board that vessel."

The packet ships made regular mail and parcel deliveries between ports, and the larger towns had them going in and out more frequently.

"That sounds perfect," said Adam. "You should certainly be back with Catherine and little Will before December."

"Lord willing," Will said. "I just hope we don't run into any weather like what we had on the way down here."

"Hopefully not."

"Have you seen Laney?"

Adam made a confused face. "Today?" He shook his head. "No, I just got here. I haven't seen Laney since we left on Sunday."

"You should probably speak to her before you return to the warehouse. I'm sure she'd be glad to see you."

"I'd love to. Where is she now?"

"I think she's in the study reading."

Will stood and walked to the doorway of the room and looked out into the foyer. Adam could hear him say, "Annabelle, would you please tell my sister she has a visitor?"

While they waited for Laney to join them in the parlor, Will said, "I want to ask you a favor. Please look after my sister when I leave. She's been through quite a bit lately. It might be a small thing compared to what others have experienced, but it's a lot for her."

Adam nodded. "You can count on me."

Just then, Laney stood at the entrance of the room. "Oh, Adam. Hello."

Adam stood and bowed his head in courtesy at her. "How do you do, Miss Laney?" He was amused to take such a formal approach to the greeting considering all they had recently gone through together.

"I'm just fine. You came to see me?"

Adam gave a nod. "Yes, ma'am. Well, you, and I wanted to check on things with your brother before he leaves tomorrow morning. Are you planning to come with him to the warehouse to see him off? If so, you know I'll be happy to bring you home afterwards."

Laney looked at her brother and then back at Adam. "Hmm… No, I think I'll probably just say my farewells here. No need to trouble you with having to bring me back."

Adam shook his head. "It's no trouble at all. I'd welcome the chance to do that for you."

All of a sudden, Laney's face seemed to indicate she was angry about something, even though her manner of speaking was still just as sweet natured as she was apt to be.

"Listen, Adam, I really appreciate you doing favors for my brother and all, and I know he's asked you to look after me when he leaves, but I've been getting along here just fine on my own these last couple of years." She looked at her brother. "There's really no need for you to both be treating me like I'm some child." She looked again at Adam. "If you want to come for a visit sometimes, by all means, please do it, but for goodness' sake don't do it as a favor or some chore."

At that, Laney turned and left the room and disappeared into the house. From the sound of it, she had marched upstairs to her room.

As soon as Adam was confident she couldn't hear him, he said to Will, "What was that about?"

Will shrugged. "I don't know. I think she's upset that I'm

leaving, and maybe she regrets that she left Boston in the first place. Anyway, it's too late for that now."

"Maybe she's upset because this will be her first Christmas without having any family around. Remember, she was supposed to be in Boston with you and Catherine and the baby, but now she'll be here."

Will shook his head. "I don't think that's it. In fact, I've asked her more than once if she wants to come with me tomorrow, but over and over again she's said no. I don't know if it's because she really doesn't want to go back to Boston, or if she was just so shaken on that last trip that she's not anxious to make another one anytime soon."

Adam wrinkled his brow in concern. "Well, you can rest easy. I'll make sure she doesn't spend Christmas alone. I know Aunt Celie will be here, and I'm guessing Charles Jr. and Annabelle are staying for a while, but I know my mother and Valentine would love to have her come spend Christmas at the tavern, or maybe some of us will come out here on Christmas to spend the day with her. And now that I think about it, Martin's her cousin and he's still here, and by Christmas he and Jenny *should* be married."

"Should be? What does that mean?"

Adam explained to Will what had happened with the Greene brothers, and that Martin was now nervous they might try to stop him and Jenny from being able to have their wedding. Will was visibly saddened to hear about this, especially considering he would be leaving the next day.

"Listen," he said, "I'm going to do something, but I don't want you to say a single word to Martin about it. Do you hear me? Not a single word!"

Adam nodded. "Of course. What is it?"

Will took a deep breath and sighed, then said, "Given the circumstances, I'm going to give you a note that should cover the bond—"

Adam's eyes widened.

"*But* I do not want you to use that money to secure a marriage license for him unless *all other options* fail. In other words, this is only for use in case of extraordinary circumstances. From what you've told me, I don't think what the Greene brothers are attempting will be an impediment for his marriage to Jenny, but just in case something else *does* come up, this is the best I can do."

"Gracious! Well, I know he'll be grateful for that, and don't worry, I won't even let him know it's an option unless every other path becomes unavailable to him."

"Promise me," said Will. "I think it's important that Martin is able to achieve this entirely on his own merits. If one of us swoops in now to rescue him from having to do this the normal way, he'll always doubt himself and wonder if he could've had a normal wedding at all."

Adam nodded. "That makes plenty of sense. It's a fair argument, and I wholeheartedly agree."

"Assuming they are able to go through with the marriage in the normal way, give him and Jenny the money as a wedding present from me and Laney and our family."

"I'll do it," said Adam.

"Good," said Will. "Let's shake on it." He extended his hand to shake Adam's.

As he was about to show Adam out, he told him that he'd bring the note in an envelope when he came to the warehouse in the morning, and that he needed to make some arrangements first.

They said their farewells, and Adam was soon on his way back to town.

WHEN HE RETURNED FROM LENNOXVILLE Point, Adam went upstairs to the living quarters. He was pleasantly surprised that Emmanuel had cooked supper, and he and Boaz were already almost done. It was nothing fancy, just a pot of clam chowder, but that, along with what was left from the loaf of bread they'd had at breakfast, made a hearty meal.

While they sat around the kitchen table and ate, they talked about the events of the day, like how much easier it was this time to get the filled casks back to the warehouse from the Wiggins's place, as well as Adam and Martin's visit with the Reverend Miller.

"You know, while we're on the subject," said Adam as though a thought just occurred to him, "I think I may have an idea that could help get Martin out of trouble."

Boaz let out a loud "Ha!" and then said, "That's a big idea you've got if you can get Martin Smith out of trouble!"

Adam and Emmanuel chuckled.

"Well, maybe at least for the time being," Adam said. "I mean, I have an idea that might help both with the Greene brothers' objection to Martin and Jenny's marriage, *and* to shut down any complaints they might bring to the constable."

Emmanuel folded his hands on the table in front of him. "So, what's this idea?"

"I was thinking if Martin and I could just go to—"

"No! Absolutely not!" his grandfather interrupted him. "You are not going *anywhere* for some time."

Adam was taken aback by Emmanuel's reaction. "But I am only talking about going down to the White Oak River...

down to Cedar Point. It's not that far! I heard earlier in the week that those gypsies ended up setting up camp down there. They decided not to go to Charleston until the spring at the earliest."

"New Bern isn't far either, but when you left to go there a month and a half ago, you somehow ended up in Boston. No, you have no business leaving Beaufort, end of story. Martin is going to have to sort these matters out for himself!"

At that moment, Boaz did something that nearly caused Adam to fall out of his chair.

"What if I go with 'em?" he said. "Might not be a bad idea."

Emmanuel looked as shocked as Adam felt. "You? Go with Adam and Martin? You do realize he means he'd sail there. Water would be involved. A boat." Emmanuel rolled his hand up and down in front of him. "Wind and waves."

Everyone knew Boaz did not do well on boats.

Boaz shrugged. "Not necessarily. We could take the horse and cart. If we find 'em, we can either have the old gypsy woman ride with us, or she could follow us back."

Emmanuel said, "That's quite a long way to ride. Too far for Rex, I'd say."

Adam couldn't believe it, but he wasn't going to stare a gift horse in the mouth. "I bet Martin would volunteer Whisky. He's young and full of energy and vitality. It's only about twenty or so miles west. Not counting the ferry across the Newport River, the trip should take about four or five hours one way."

Boaz nodded. "And if we left tomorrow after the *Gypsy* departs, I reckon we should easily be back by Saturday evening, or maybe even Friday, with time to spare."

Emmanuel narrowed his eyes and shook his head. He looked like he was in utter disbelief.

"Listen," said Boaz, "those Greene boys are hell-bent on causing trouble. At the very least, we can get Martin out of town for a couple of days and maybe—"

"Wait just a minute," Emmanuel interrupted. "Even if I approved of this little journey, I hardly think it's a wise idea to take Martin with you. I seem to remember hearing that the old gypsy woman wasn't too fond of him... Something about her daughter."

"True," said Adam. "Martin doesn't have to go. In fact, he can stay here and keep you company. It'll be good for him."

"Ha!" Boaz chuckled. "That does sound like a good idea. Maybe you can dispense some of your wisdom to him while he's here."

Adam nodded in agreement. Emmanuel brushed his hand in front of him dismissively.

"So?" said Adam.

"So what?" Emmanuel replied.

"Will you let us go?"

There was a long, silent pause, and then his grandfather finally let out a big sigh and said, "I suppose, *but* on the condition you wait and leave Friday. You should get an early start. Furthermore, I know if you have your mind on leaving after the *Gypsy* departs tomorrow you'll rush through loading and make a mess of things."

Chapter Seven

IT WAS A GOOD THING Emmanuel insisted that Adam and Boaz wait until Friday to leave. For one thing, it took until after lunch to get the *Gypsy* underway. After that, it started raining early that evening and didn't stop until close to midnight. Fortunately, on Friday morning the sun was out and the weather was fair—around sixty degrees— not bad for late November.

Martin arrived at the warehouse that morning to clean up from the previous day's work. He said to Adam he looked forward to staying with Emmanuel until Adam and Boaz returned.

"I'll try not to get him into too much mischief," he joked, elbowing Emmanuel in the ribs, as they all walked outside the street-side bay doors to the waiting horse and cart.

Emmanuel elbowed him back, then shook his head in amusement.

Adam gave a little laugh as he loaded his sack into the cart and climbed up, followed by Boaz. "Well, you keep yourself out of mischief too," said Adam. "We're doing this to help you get out of this mess you're in so you can marry your girl. Just don't make anything worse."

Emmanuel was standing nearby and made his eyes big

and gave a nod in amused agreement. He then tipped his head towards Martin. "I'll keep him out of trouble," he assured them.

Martin grinned, and then he reached up and shook hands with Adam and Boaz. "I really do appreciate this, y'all. Take good care of Whisky." He walked towards the horse's head and gave him a pat.

Adam said, "Will do."

Boaz gave Martin a nod.

Soon, Adam and Boaz were on their way to the ferry that crossed the Newport River, on the northwest side of town.

Once they were across, they made good time. Including a few breaks for the horse and for themselves to stretch their legs, they made it to the gypsy camp in five hours.

IT TURNED OUT THAT MADAME Endora and the gypsy camp had not even gone as far as Cedar Point. They were a few miles east of there, and they had set up their camp along a sparsely populated stretch of land on Bogue Sound. Everything looked similar to the way it had when the gypsies were camped in Beaufort, only Adam thought it was interesting that there weren't signs advertising fortune-telling or potions, and there didn't appear to be any sign of the acrobatics that attracted so may Beaufort residents.

The old woman's tent was easy to spot. It was larger than the others, and it had a few peaks in its roof from where there were multiple poles inside holding it up. Adam guessed it was necessarily larger than the other tents because she conducted her divination business inside, so she frequently had paying guests. As Adam and Boaz approached the tent, though, he heard what sounded like an old woman singing on the other side of it. The two walked around and saw Madame Endora stirring something in a big, black cast-iron pot that was hanging over a fire while singing some song that Adam didn't recognize.

"Ma'am," said Adam to get her attention.

She looked up from her cooking, visibly stunned. "It is you!" She didn't look pleased in the slightest.

Adam, on the other hand, was happy to see her. "You remember me! I'm so glad we found you!"

She looked at him as if he were crazy.

Adam was unfazed. "Listen," he said, "I know this is going to sound strange, but we need you to come back to Beaufort with us—that is, if you're willing."

Madame Endora looked at Adam in disbelief.

"Surely you are joking, boy," she said, her thick accent exactly the way he remembered it. "I did not think we have anything to talk about since I last saw you."

Adam shook his head. "No, I'm not joking. We need you to come and be a witness for us... for a friend."

She raised an eyebrow. "A friend?" she said. "What friend? I have no friends there. Remember, your lawman told me to leave and never to return."

Adam hung his head and sighed. He remembered when Constable Squires said those exact words to her, but that didn't matter now.

"I know," Adam said in acknowledgement, "but whoever thought we would need you as a witness? This is a different situation. And we'll speak up on your behalf if anyone gives you any trouble."

Boaz nodded in agreement. "That's right, ma'am.

Constable Squires is my cousin. I can personally assure you that you will be in no legal trouble if you return."

Madame Endora cocked her head back and tsk-tsked in skepticism.

"Listen," said Adam, "my friend—he could really use your help. He's just trying to clear his name for an awful thing he's been accused of doing, and you can help him do that. You owe it to him!"

"Your friend?" The gypsy woman's eyes grew as round as saucers. "Is this the same *friend* who tried to defile my daughter?"

Adam took a deep breath before responding. "Yes, ma'am, that's the one." He paused, and then he said, "But to be fair, you nearly killed him with that nasty concoction you told me to give him."

Madame Endora nodded in concession to his point. "This is true, but he is a man who deserved it."

Adam thought she looked just a tiny bit ashamed, but he wasn't going to argue with a mother who likely felt justified in defending her daughter's virtue.

"Maybe so," he said. "But why don't we just agree that things are even between the two of you now?"

She narrowed her eyes and looked doubtful. Adam waited for her response.

Suddenly, a voice came from behind Adam. "Mama, you should go with him. It is the right thing to do."

Adam turned around and saw Madame Endora's oldest daughter, Stela. The raven-haired beauty was just as mesmerizing as she had been that first time he had seen her at the gypsy camp on the north side of Town Creek. Her hair was loosely piled up on her head, and wavy tendrils fell around her face and spilled over her collarbones.

No sooner had Adam taken in her beauty, he felt guilty for noticing. It never occurred to him that he'd see her again, but something about her certainly was captivating.

Madame Endora spoke and broke his wandering train of thought.

"What is it you need from me?" she asked.

Adam smiled. "Do you remember the man that came and asked you to put a curse on Martin?"

Endora gave a single deep nod and said, "Big, tall man? Lots of…" She held up her arms as though she were flexing her biceps.

Adam nodded.

"I do," she said.

"Well, his name was Hardy Greene. He's dead now."

The woman looked stunned.

Adam quickly continued. "You see, when the constable and Jones and I got back to Beaufort after we had found you near Broad Creek, we got the news that Hardy died several hours earlier."

Madame Endora looked concerned but also confused.

"Here is where our problem comes: his brothers are now trying to accuse my friend Martin of hiring you to put a curse on him, and they're saying that might've killed him."

The woman's jaw dropped and her eyes bulged.

"What? But that is not true! And I am not even able to curse a man to death. It is just an act!"

"I know that," said Adam, "but that is what Hardy's brothers are saying, so they are trying to claim that Martin had a role in Hardy Greene's death, and that at the very least he's guilty of attempted murder."

Madame Endora had a look of disgust, and she brushed her hand in the air in front of her face dismissively. "That is ridiculous."

"I *agree* with you, but that's why we need you to come to Beaufort yourself, so you can testify to that effect—at least tell the authorities what you know."

Adam and Boaz had already decided on their way to Cedar Point that they wouldn't go into too many details, such as the fact that she might need to talk to both the Reverend and the magistrate.

She rested her hands on her hips and looked down, then shook her head. "No. No, I do not think the people in your town will like to see us there. I would think they all know about the empty barrel now, and that we had no girl buried in their graveyard. They will not trust us. It is better for us that we do not go."

"You don't all have to go," said Boaz. "If you want, just you can go. We'll bring you back."

"Or bring your daughters if you would prefer. But certainly, you don't need to *all* go back to Beaufort." Adam waved his hand around, indicating all of the gypsies at the camp. "That would certainly draw more attention than just the three of you."

"That's true," said Boaz. "And don't worry about anybody even knowing you're there. Fletcher's family has a tavern. They can put you up in a room, and no one will even have to find out you're in town."

Adam flashed Boaz a look of shock. He couldn't believe he had offered the hospitality of the Topsail Tavern without discussing it with him first. Valentine was no fan of gypsies, so there was no telling how he'd take the news that he'd need to put the strange visitors up for a couple of nights.

Nevertheless, soon all had agreed that Madame Endora and her daughters would be following Adam and Boaz back to Beaufort.

ADAM KNEW BETTER THAN TO lead the gypsy women through the front door of the tavern, so he took them directly to the back. He sent Boaz in the front to tell either Mary or Valentine to go to the kitchen and meet him there.

Aunt Franny was kneading dough when the group came in the back door. The startled woman straightened her back and gave Adam a puzzled look, but before she said anything, Adam said, "Evening, Aunt Franny. Sorry to disturb you. I expect my mother or Valentine to be back here directly."

"Hmph." She went back to work, only kneading the dough a bit more slowly, looking up every so often.

Adam could tell she was trying not to make a face, but he knew what she was likely thinking. Valentine was *not* going to like this.

He motioned towards a chair and a couple of crates for Madame Endora and her daughters to sit, if they desired. Madame Endora took the chair, but the girls remained standing.

It only took a minute or two before Mary came through the door into the kitchen, but it felt like twenty minutes. "Boaz just told me you—" She stopped short as soon as she saw the visitors.

"Mama, you remember Madame Endora."

The old woman nodded her head in courtesy.

Adam motioned to the young women. "And these are her daughters, Stela and Aurora."

Stela was about the same age as Adam, and Aurora seemed to be two or three years younger. With their dark features and bohemian fashion sense, there was no doubt they were sisters.

Mary's jaw was slack. She finally was able to muster out a "How do you do?"

"How do you do?" Madame Endora and the girls responded with a nod, almost in unison.

Mary stepped over and grabbed Adam by his upper arm hard.

She pulled him aside and whispered fiercely, "Have you lost your mind? Does Valentine know about this?"

Adam shook his head and whispered in response, "No, and neither did I until Boaz sprang this on me yesterday evening."

"Why are they here?" Mary asked.

"It's a long story, but the main thing is they are here to testify about a matter, but we don't want the whole town to know they're here. Boaz suggested they might stay until they speak to the magistrate, and then they can leave just as quietly as they came."

Mary's wrinkled brow betrayed her concern.

"Don't worry," Adam said. "I'll explain everything to Valentine, and we'll pay him double for the room, but where else can they stay without anyone finding out?"

"I don't mind them being here. Remember, I visited the old woman twice when they were in town, but Valentine…"

"Can you just give me a key to one of the upstairs rooms so I can take them up the back stairs and get them settled in? And maybe you can bring them something to eat."

Mary looked over at the exotic travelers, then back at Adam. She gave a quick sigh and pressed her lips together as she seemed to be thinking about how to handle this.

"You think there's any chance Valentine doesn't even have to know they're here?" Adam suggested.

"I don't know. But I'll do what I can for them. Hang on, and I'll get you a key to the room right across from our room."

Adam thought it was kind of sweet that his mother still referred to the room he was raised in as "our" room, even though he hadn't lived in it for a couple of years now.

She disappeared back out into the dining room and was back within seconds with the key. He leaned over and gave his mother a kiss on the cheek and thanked her, then took the women upstairs and showed them to their room.

"Listen," he told them. "I cannot stress to you how important it is that you stay *very* quiet. You cannot be up here dancing and making a bunch of noise. There may be other guests in the adjacent rooms, and we're trying to get you in and out of town without drawing attention to your presence."

Stela stood, hands on her hips, and said, "Dancing and making a bunch of noise? We do not just go around dancing and making noise everywhere we go. What a ridiculous idea!"

Adam didn't care that she was offended by his admonition. He didn't want to take any chances by not warning them. He hoped the women might stay quiet enough that they would remain undetected by Valentine. If and when the tavern keeper found out they were staying upstairs, he'd surely have something to say about it—and it wouldn't be polite.

"When I go back downstairs, I'll ask Aunt Franny to

put together some supper for you and to bring it up. Don't bother putting your tray outside the door when you're done. My mother will likely collect them herself in the morning, or Aunt Franny will do it."

"Will I speak to the lawman first thing tomorrow?" Madame Endora asked.

Adam shook his head. "Well, tomorrow's Sunday. I doubt he'll be working tomorrow, but I'd think Monday."

"Monday?"

Adam nodded. "I'm not sure when he'll be able to see you, if it will be early in the morning or later in the day, but I can't imagine he'd make you wait too long, given the circumstances."

"What will you have us do tomorrow? Will we just wait in this same room?"

"Yes, please. It won't be very long. Everyone will be at church tomorrow. In fact, Hardy Greene's brothers might be there to make their complaint about Martin."

Madame Endora looked at her daughters in bewilderment. "What kind of people are these?" She turned her attention back to Adam. "You people accuse others of crimes right in the church? Then I am glad I do not go to church!"

Adam shook his head. "No, ma'am, you don't understand. If they made that accusation of Martin, that would just be their way of making an objection. Tomorrow is the first Sunday that the banns will be read."

"The banns? What is this?" Her eyes grew wide.

"Wedding banns. Martin is getting married to the widow of Hardy Greene."

"I know what these wedding banns are! So this man's brothers, they are angry your friend is marrying their dead brother's wife. And their brother was mad at your friend also, and this is why he was asking me to curse him. True?"

Adam nodded. "Yes, something like that."

Endora cocked her head back and looked at him skeptically. "What did your friend do to make the dead man hate him so much?"

Adam took a deep breath and debated whether or not to answer the old woman's question, but ultimately he decided to, but just not go into all of the details.

"Martin and Hardy Greene's widow, Jenny, were sweethearts when they were younger, but Hardy asked her to marry him before Martin ever did. The problem was, even though Jenny married Hardy, he was not a very nice man—not to her, not to anybody—and she still loved Martin."

"Ah," said Endora, "so your friend, he was involved with this Hardy Greene's wife, so he wanted me to curse your friend to death, but instead Hardy Green drops dead himself."

"Yep. That's pretty much the way it happened."

"I see... Then for some reason the Fates wanted your friend and this girl to end up together, or at least it appears this way, yes?"

Adam shrugged. "I don't believe in 'the Fates,' but yes, I suppose you could say it appears that way."

"Hmph." Madame Endora clutched her bag as she studied the room. She stopped and gave a disapproving look at the chimney. "It is cold in this room. There is no fire, and there is no wood."

"No, ma'am," Adam said. "But I can bring you some wood and help you get a fire started if you'd like. They don't keep fires burning in empty rooms."

He was caught a little bit off guard by her sudden change of subject.

"Tell me what happens in your church if these men stand up tomorrow and say this false accusation."

"Well"—Adam thought for a moment—"to tell you the truth, I'm not sure exactly. But I know the Reverend will allow them to voice their objection. I guess then we'll just have to see what happens."

She nodded, then turned her attention back to the chimney. "Where is the wood?"

"Just downstairs, out back. Right by the door where we came in. I'm happy to go get you some."

"My daughters can go get the wood. We are not helpless women."

Adam shook his head. "I'm sure you're not, but I'd be happy to go get wood for your fire."

Madame Endora made a hand motion to her daughters, who immediately stepped towards the door.

Stela said, "Excuse me." She waited for Adam to let her pass by.

"Just a minute," Adam said, holding up his finger. "I understand that you women are used to taking care of things for yourselves, but I think it's best if you just stay here. If you need anything, someone will be up to check on you every few hours or so, or if it's an emergency, just send one of the girls down to the kitchen, but please be discreet about it."

"The back of this inn is very private," argued Madame Endora. "Who will see my girls just going down to get wood? I see no need for us to be confined only to this tiny room."

Adam took a deep breath, then let out a sigh. First of all, he didn't think the rooms were so tiny. He had grown up in one the same size until he was seventeen. Next, since the women wouldn't be staying at the Topsail very long, he didn't think there should be any problem with them staying out of sight.

"Please do not worry," Stela said. "No one will see us. We can move very quickly and very quietly."

These women were used to making the whole world their home, living in tents, traveling from place to place—even across the sea—so he tried to remind himself that they might truly be bothered by such confinement.

Finally, he gave a nod. "Fine. You two can go get the wood, but please, please, *please* don't let anyone see you."

Stela and Aurora both shook their heads, and then they quickly scurried down the hall towards the kitchen. Adam bade Madame Endora farewell and then left towards the stairs that led into the dining room so he could meet up with Boaz.

"Where'd you come from?" Valentine said. He looked up at Adam from over the top of his spectacles.

The sixtysomething-year-old tavern keeper was sitting behind the bar and studying the ledger.

Adam had to think on his feet. "Oh, I had gone upstairs from the kitchen to take care of something for Mama but just decided to come back down this way, since Bo said he'd be waiting here."

Valentine nodded. "Is that right? Hmm." He gave Adam a nod, and then he looked back down at the book and traced his finger down the page to where he had apparently been studying before.

Adam looked over Valentine's head and saw his mother pouring drinks for some men at the bar. She shook her head and mouthed something at him, but he didn't understand.

Valentine hadn't seen her, so Adam gave his head a quick, tiny shake, and then discreetly shrugged his shoulders. He mouthed, "What?"

His mother pointed at Valentine and then mouthed something else, but Adam was still perplexed.

"Well, Mama, we better go. We promised Emmanuel we'd get back as quick as we could. I reckon I'll probably see you tomorrow after church."

Mary smiled and nodded. She gave a strange look in Valentine's direction, but Adam had no idea what she was trying to indicate. She then tipped her head, as if to tell him to ask Boaz.

Adam and Boaz walked towards the door of the tavern, but just before they opened it, Valentine said, "You get that room good and warm for the guests?"

Adam's heart fell to his stomach. *That* was what his mother was trying to tell him. Valentine knew.

He glanced at Boaz, then at his mother, then at Valentine, who was resting his elbow on the bar and stroking the mostly white, but reddish, stubble on his face. He was looking at Adam in a way he hadn't seen in a *very* long time.

Adam crossed right over to the bar. "You know?"

The old man gave a deep nod. "I do."

"Who told you?"

Valentine looked over Adam's shoulder towards Boaz.

Adam looked back. "You told him?"

"It's easier that way," he said. "He understands. And he understands he'll be paid for the trouble."

Adam turned his head and looked back at his mother and Valentine. "And that's all there is to it?"

"Oh, I'm not happy about it," said Valentine, "but it

seems I've been left with little choice. That's alright, though. I'll fix you for it."

Adam closed his eyes and tilted his head upward and took a deep breath. *God only knows what that means.* He knew Valentine well enough to know he wasn't *really* mad, but he was aggravated, and now it was anyone's guess what he might do to get Adam back—and by getting him back, that typically meant playing a trick on him in some way, or embarrassing him.

He waved at Valentine and his mother, and then he and Boaz left the tavern and returned to the warehouse.

Chapter Eight

SUNDAY MORNING, EMMANUEL MADE SURE Adam and Boaz were both up early to get a fire going *and* to get ready for church. Today would be the first reading of the marriage banns between Martin and Jenny.

Adam had asked about Laney, whether she was going to be there.

"William told me that she *would* be attending for the publication of her cousin's wedding banns," said Emmanuel, "to offer him her moral support."

Laney and Will's branch of the family never made a habit of attending the services in town, as the town's church was Church of England. Her parents, on the other hand, were Baptists, and Baptists were historically not treated well by the Anglican leadership. In fact, Laney and Will had heard stories about the Baptists in Craven County being thrown into the gaol for insisting on holding unapproved services.

Laney and Will were never taken to church growing up unless they traveled to the Pamlico River with their family, as there were no regular Baptist services near Beaufort, except when an itinerant preacher came through the area. After Will moved to New Bern, Laney usually stayed home, since Lennoxville Point was quite a distance from town. She had visited on special occasions at the Anglican church from time to time, however.

Martin, on the other hand, had been attending services at the Anglican church since he began working for Emmanuel. Emmanuel always insisted that his employees go to church on Sundays. As much as it might've annoyed Martin on those mornings when he'd have preferred to sleep off his drinking from Saturday night, when Reverend Miller read the banns today, Adam suspected his friend would be happy that he had conceded to his grandfather's wishes.

"Did Will say who was going to take her?" Adam asked as he poured himself a cup of coffee. He and his grandfather were having a small breakfast of coffee and toast before church.

"Charles Jr., I believe," Emmanuel answered.

A few hours later, Emmanuel, Adam, and Boaz were in the horse cart riding through town in brisk weather. The temperature had dropped fifteen degrees overnight. They were all bundled up in wool coats, hats, and gloves. Elliot and Ricky Jones would be meeting them there. Usually, Martin sat on one of the two rows that were occupied by the men from Rogers's Shipping Company, but today he would be on the front row for when his and Jenny's names were called.

The church was more packed than usual, a welcome development given the cold temperature outside. More bodies meant more natural heat. The room seemed to warm up another five degrees for Adam when he saw Laney Martin enter the sanctuary from the vestibule. He tried to catch her attention to wave, but she made a beeline for the row right behind her cousin. She came up behind him and tapped on his shoulders. Adam could see Martin was elated that she was there. Jenny was happy to see her as well.

Everything about the service progressed as it always did, but towards the end—but just prior to the singing of the final Psalm—Reverend Miller said, "I publish the Banns of Marriage between Martin Smith, of the Town of Beaufort, and Jane Greene, of the same. If any of you know cause, or just impediment, why these two persons should not be joined together in holy matrimony, ye are to declare it. This is the first time of asking."

At that very moment, Adam heard a commotion behind him. Like clockwork, it was the Greene brothers who had both stood to lodge their protest.

The older brother, Henry, spoke. "We object, Reverend."

Martin and Jenny both looked mortified. Reverend Miller, on the other hand, seemed remarkably calm. Adam attributed that to his having been warned of this possibility beforehand.

"What is the objection?" said the preacher.

Bill pointed his finger directly at Martin and said, "That man is responsible for the death of my brother."

The entire congregation gasped. Adam and his Rogers's Shipping Company colleagues exchanged pained looks of annoyance.

"Alright," said Reverend Miller. "There is no need for anyone to be dismayed. We have an ordinary procedure for this very thing." He turned his attention to the men protesting in the back of the congregation. "Gentlemen, the elders and I would like to speak with you two in private so we can ascertain more precisely what your claim is, and we will evaluate the evidence, and of course the groom-to-be will have an opportunity to respond to any accusations. Please stay, and we'll speak after the conclusion of this service."

Henry and Bill exchanged looks as if they were checking to see if they were both in agreement. Both of them nodded at each other, and then they sat back on the row.

At that, Reverend Miller indicated they would sing the last song, and then he would give the benediction and the congregation would be dismissed.

Adam wished he could've been a fly on the wall for the conversation between Reverend Miller, the elders, and the Greene brothers, but he would have to be satisfied with learning about it after the fact.

Chapter Nine

A DAM DIDN'T HAVE TO WAIT long wondering what was said. By Sunday night, Martin rode Whisky out to the warehouse to let him, his grandfather, and Boaz know what happened.

"The Reverend says if I have any witnesses, he'd like very much to speak with them," said Martin. "So I reckon that means somebody ought to carry that gypsy woman out there to talk to him tomorrow."

"I'll do it," said Adam. "Do you mind if I take Rex and the cart?" he asked his grandfather.

"Of course not, but handle it early in the morning. The sooner this matter is sorted out, the better."

The next morning after breakfast, instead of going down to the warehouse to work, Adam was given leave to go to the tavern and transport Madame Endora to the church. When Adam told her where he needed to take her, she seemed visibly nervous. As they pulled up in front of the rectory, Adam noticed she was gripping the little purse she was carrying so hard her knuckles were white.

He turned to her and gave her a little smile and a small nod. "It's going to be just fine. Reverend Miller is a nice man. All you have to do is tell the truth."

She grabbed his arm before they climbed out of the cart. "From now on, please, I am just Endora, not Madame Endora."

Adam wasn't quite sure why she said that, but he smiled and said, "Alright."

A couple of minutes later, Adam and Endora were sitting in the parlor with the Reverend Miller, who had just requested his housekeeper to fix a pot of tea for his guests.

"Well, madam, I do appreciate your willingness to come and speak with me today. I understand you had to travel quite a ways to make yourself available in this matter."

Endora looked at Adam as though she was waiting for him to indicate she should speak. He just gave a subtle little nod and mouthed, "It's fine."

"Yes, sir," she said. "My family and I, we are living right now about five hours west of here on Bogue Sound, a few miles east of the White Oak River."

"I see, and do you have a large family?"

"Well, my *whole* family"—she flopped out both hands as she answered—"yes, very large. But my own family is just me and my two granddaughters."

"Your granddaughters?" Adam asked. "Stela and Aurora? I thought they were your daughters."

"I have taken care of them their whole lives. I have raised them. They are like my daughters to me, but to be very truthful, they are my granddaughters." She motioned to Reverend Miller. "This is a holy man, so I must tell him exactly the truth." Adam noticed she looked at the large Bible on the table near where the Reverend was sitting before she continued, this time speaking again directly to the Reverend. "My own daughter was their mother, but she ran away with a man who belonged to a traveling troupe of trick riders right after Aurora was born."

Gracious, if that doesn't beat all I've ever heard, thought Adam.

"God bless you, dear woman," said the Reverend. "What a kind and generous thing you did taking in your granddaughters and giving them a happy home all of this time. Some less caring souls might've turned them out as orphans."

Adam noticed Endora grip her purse in front of her again, but this time with a look of pride on her face.

"I could never do such a thing, sir. So I have made the girls my own daughters, and now I take care of them the best way that I can."

"Is your husband living?" asked the Reverend.

"No," she said stoically. "He died right after my only daughter was born."

"And you never married again?" The Reverend seemed surprised.

"No, my husband was not so nice when he was living, so I was not interested in having another one."

"Fair enough. So you have managed all of these years, then, to care for your granddaughters on your own?"

She nodded. "Mostly, yes. Sometimes brothers or sisters have helped, but I work to earn money so I can take care of us."

"Is that a fact? And what exactly do you do?"

"I tell fortunes." She looked nervous as she answered. She glanced at Adam, then looked down at the floor, then back at the Reverend. "I do not *really* tell fortunes, if I am telling you the truth. I make a show. I am like"—she seemed to be searching for the word—"an actress. I have a tent and I make it look very mysterious, and then my daughter—my grand-daughter Stela—she stands outside and takes the money and sends people in with different kinds of stones or objects so I know then what to tell them."

Reverend Miller wrinkled his brow. "Huh. And how exactly does that work?"

Adam wondered the same thing, because he thought Endora's fortune for him did have some elements of truth. He was very curious to know what she'd say.

"Well." She thought for a moment. "For instance, when you came to have me tell your fortune"—she raised her finger towards Adam—"my Stela sent you back with two stones: a turquoise, and a small, round crystal."

Adam nodded. "That's right." He was a little bit embarrassed that this was all coming out right in front of the Reverend, but his interest in hearing about her methods overpowered his embarrassment. "I figured the small, round crystal just meant I wanted a crystal ball reading."

"Yes, that is exactly right," she said, "but the other stone, like I said, was a turquoise, which means you had mentioned something to Stela about someone from very far away in another part of the world."

Adam tried to think back and remember. Yes, he had mentioned that his father was from Havana.

"Well, why did you think he was dead? I remember you said something about the person you saw in the crystal ball was no more."

"We have many different types of the same kinds of stone. The particular turquoise you brought in had a little crack that I could feel. That meant the person from far away was either dead or in parts unknown."

"How did you know it was my father?"

"That is easy," said Endora. "You asked me if it was a man or a woman. I asked you if your mother lived near here, and you said yes, so I knew there was a good chance whoever the faraway person was, was your father. Lucky guess."

"That's it? That's how you came up with that whole story?"

She nodded her head. "Yes, that is exactly how I do it."

Adam shook his head in disbelief. "Ha! I wondered about that. I was really nervous after what you said, because—"

The Reverend chuckled. "Sounds like you two could have a lively conversation about this, but how about right now we just get to the matter at hand? I don't want to trouble this dear lady for any more of her time than is necessary."

Endora sat up a little straighter and held her chin up a bit, indicating she was happily awaiting whatever question the Reverend had for her. Adam was amused.

"Madam, do you remember when Martin Smith came to see you at the camp?"

"I do."

"Would you mind telling me exactly what happened that evening?"

"I would be happy to. This Martin Smith…" She looked at Adam and said, "This is your friend? The one with the curly blond hair, yes?"

Adam nodded.

"Alright, good. I just do not want to confuse these two men that we are needing to talk about. This Martin Smith paid my Stela for a full fortune-telling. He wanted my whole bag of tricks, we might say."

"And did you tell him a fortune?"

"I told him what I tell all of the excited young men and women who come to see me for the expensive fortune—that all of his dreams will come true, that he will marry the most beautiful woman, and that he has a future ahead of him that though it might have its trials, will turn out to be one that brings great joy."

"I see," said Reverend Miller. "And did he ask you anything else? Did he have any other services he wanted you to perform?"

Endora made a face at him as though she wasn't sure if she should be offended by his question.

"What I'm asking is, Did he ask you to put a curse on anybody?"

"No! He did not! The only man who came to the camp while we were here and asked me to make a curse was the big strong man." She thought for a second. "What is his name?" she asked Adam.

"Hardy Greene."

"Yes, this Hardy Greene. He said that a man was his worst rival, and that he hated him and he wondered if I will put a curse on him."

"And did you?" asked the Reverend.

"I cannot make curses any more than I can see the future," she said. "But I asked him how much it was worth to him to do this thing. He said five pounds. That is a lot of money to me. I looked at him like this." She gave the Reverend a wink and a nod. "And then I held out my palm like this." She held her palm out in front of her, as though she were waiting for the Reverend to put something in it. "And then he put money in my hand, and that was it."

"That was *it*?" Adam asked, stunned. "He gave you five

pounds and didn't even make sure that you were going to actually give him what he was paying you for?"

"Well," she said, "to tell you the truth, I think he was nervous. I think he knew he was doing something not right, and he did not want to get caught."

"Alright then," said the Reverend. "So, just to be clear, you never have actually done any fortune-telling or cast any curses, correct?"

"That is correct, but if people hear this, I will go out of business, just so you know."

"My dear lady," said the Reverend, "I cannot begin to tell you how helpful you have been by coming here today. Truly. You seem like a delightful person, and I really would like to get to know you better. I have a favor to ask."

Endora wrinkled her brow. She looked at Adam. She seemed a little bit apprehensive, but Adam shrugged. He didn't know what the Reverend was going to say. She then turned her attention back to the Reverend. "What is it?"

"You may have heard that yesterday was the first reading of the wedding banns for Martin Smith and his bride-to-be, Jane—they call her Jenny—Greene. The whole reason we needed you to come here was because the brothers of Hardy Greene, Jane Greene's late husband, stood before the congregation after the banns were read and accused Martin Smith of trying to have their brother killed."

"And I already told you that is not what happened. It was the Greene man who wanted the cursing."

"Yes, madam, so what I would like to ask, if you wouldn't mind, is please come with Adam to church next Sunday, and possibly the following. You needn't stand up and say anything, but then if any of the elders wish to speak to you after the service, they can, and you can tell them what you told me—just the part about Hardy Greene asking for the curse and not Martin."

She placed her hand on her chest and looked confused. "You want *me* to come to your church?"

"Yes, madam, if it isn't too much of an imposition. It might possibly help this wrongly accused young man to clear his name—in this circumstance, anyway—and it will certainly make his bride-to-be happy."

Endora took a deep breath. She looked like she was considering it.

"I should tell you, sir, that I have never been to a Sunday church service. Is there anything I should know? Is there anything special I will have to do?"

"I'll tell you what. I have an extra copy of a book—it is the copy I usually keep here in the parlor for parishioners to look over while we're planning special services, but it is called the Book of Common Prayer."

He held the book open and turned to a page somewhere in the middle, and then he handed it to her. She took it and began flipping through the pages before she said, "I do not read."

"That's quite alright, madam. I'm sure Adam here can help explain it all to you. I think it might comfort you a bit that in that book you'll be able to see exactly what will happen in our service on Sunday and what we will be talking about from the pulpit. It is the second Sunday of Advent. That means we are only two more Sundays past this one away from Christmas, which is when we celebrate the coming of our blessed Savior, Jesus Christ."

Endora looked bewildered.

"I'll help her with that, Reverend," said Adam. "So, does that take care of everything here today?"

"It does, thank you," he said. The Reverend stood and bade Adam and Endora farewell, and he said to her, "I truly do look forward to seeing you in my congregation on the next Lord's Day."

AFTER TAKING ENDORA BACK TO the Topsail Tavern, Adam returned to the warehouse. He could hardly wait to tell his grandfather about the conversation between Reverend Miller and the old woman.

"I was just amazed," Adam said as he sat in sitting room of the living quarters with Emmanuel and recounted some of the most memorable moments in the exchange. "She has always come across as so stiff necked, so independent, but her manner just changed *completely* in front of the Reverend."

Emmanuel shrugged. "Well, you did say she called him a 'holy man.' Perhaps she has a reverence for a man of the cloth, or perhaps it's more rooted in superstition, but nevertheless, it's a good thing she was gracious rather than stubborn."

"Oh, I agree," said Adam, "but I was just as surprised by how gracious Reverend Miller was with her. She was sitting right there admitting to deceiving people by selling them her made-up fortunes and even letting a man believe she would curse his adversary, but Reverend Miller didn't act even a little bit startled by any of it. On the contrary, he spoke to her with the kindness one might have with a little child who believes in fairy stories."

"Good heavens," said Emmanuel. "Why would that surprise you? Because he wouldn't have had the same response to you if you had told him you'd done something similar?"

"I reckon."

"Adam, you are and have been a faithful member of his flock for over two years now. His expectations of you are different, since you have knowledge and understanding about the Scriptures that Madame Endora does not. She, on the other hand, has never even attended Sunday services, you said. It's right that he would speak to her with great gentleness and show her compassion, as he can't expect her to live and act like a Christian if she is not one."

"Well, she may not be one yet, but I think if the Reverend has his way she will be before it's all over with. He's invited her and her granddaughters to church on Sunday."

"Her granddaughters?"

"Oh, that's another thing! She said Stela and Aurora were actually born to her daughter, but her daughter took off, and so she ended up raising them like her daughters. I suppose that makes sense. She did seem a bit aged to have such young daughters."

"Hmm… There's no telling what if any effect attending services at the church will have on Endora and her granddaughters, but don't forget that ultimately God is sovereign over all things, and if He's purposed to save them, nothing and no one can thwart His will. But don't assume the worst if they leave Beaufort and return to their camp seemingly unchanged. You never know what seeds might have been planted."

When Sunday arrived, Adam, Emmanuel, and Boaz stopped by the tavern and picked up Endora, Stela, and Aurora, and they all rode in the cart to church. The group sat on the usual pews where the men from Rogers's Shipping Company sat. Adam looked for Laney to enter the sanctuary again, as he wanted to introduce her to Endora and her granddaughters, but she didn't arrive until just before the service started. She did turn and look in his direction as she came into the sanctuary. He waved and smiled at her, but she hurriedly sat down behind Martin and Jenny, just as she had done the previous Sunday.

Everyone was relieved when the service ended and the Greene brothers never appeared. Adam and Martin had talked about it the night before. Martin had heard that the Reverend and the elders were unimpressed with their accusations, and the Reverend apparently was able to inform the elders about what Endora had said so that they were satisfied about the matter. She never did have to appear before the magistrate, but then again, if Peter Robins, who attended the same church, saw that the matter was of no concern to the clergy, then it was unlikely he would've been moved to take action against Martin based on the word of Hardy Greene's brothers.

Endora and her granddaughters also attended the church service the following Sunday, which was the third reading of the banns. With no further objections, the Sunday after that one the wedding would be solemnized.

Adam had already convinced Valentine to have a special supper party at the Topsail Tavern to celebrate the happy occasion the evening after the wedding.

Chapter Ten

A FEW HOURS AFTER MARTIN and Jenny's wedding, Adam hurriedly finished up the last details at the Topsail Tavern before the newlyweds arrived. The mistletoe was in place to greet them as they came through the front door, and Adam secretly hoped he might have a chance to steal a kiss from Laney when she arrived.

He was dressed his very best. The feast was prepared, and the Topsail Tavern looked beautiful. It should be a perfect night, he thought.

Some of the smaller tables had been rearranged to form one long table that ran between the staircase and the fireplace. There was room to seat eighteen altogether, although Adam wasn't sure that many would attend.

Adam had hired a couple of local musicians to perform for the party. One man played the fiddle, while the other something like a small guitar. They had entertained at the Topsail Tavern in the past, but they had since taken to playing elsewhere. Valentine thought they were charging too much.

"They've gotten too big for their britches," he had said.

Fortunately, since Emmanuel had contributed greatly to the expenses for the evening's festivities, Adam paid them out of the allocated budget.

The only thing Adam was nervous about was what Laney would think of the gypsy guests. After all, she had been in Boston with Will and his family when the large group of gypsies were camped on the northwest edge of town, and although they had all been in the same church on the last two Sundays the banns were read, and during the wedding service that had happened earlier that day, they had never formally been introduced.

It was around six o'clock when guests began to arrive. First to arrive was Jackson, a boyhood friend of Adam and a server at the Topsail Tavern. He brought an auburn-haired young lady he introduced as Annie.

As it turned out, some of Jackson's family were already there. Valentine had asked him earlier in the week to round up a couple of servers for the party, and Jackson recruited a couple of his younger brothers.

Ricky Jones was next to arrive. "Where's my lovely young companion for the evenin?" he asked. He looked across the room until he spotted Stela. "There she is." He crossed over to greet her. "How d'ya do, ma'am?" He reached out to take her hand to kiss it.

She gave him a little curtsy, and Adam thought he saw her blush.

Emmanuel and Boaz arrived soon thereafter. Then Mary came down the stairs with Endora and Aurora. She introduced the women to the guests but left it to Adam to make the introductions with his grandfather.

He motioned first to the older woman. "I'd like you to meet Endora, and this is her granddaughter Aurora. Her eldest granddaughter, Stela, over there"—he motioned in her direction—"is Jones's supper companion for the evening."

Emmanuel gave a reserved smile and nod. "Pleased to meet you," he said.

Mary showed Emmanuel, Boaz, Endora, and Aurora to the punch bowl and hors d'oeuvres.

Next, Elliot arrived with his wife, Ana.

When is that girl going to get here? Adam kept wondering. He knew Laney had mentioned Charles Jr. would be bringing her in her carriage, but he was impatient for her to arrive. It seemed like everyone was there now except for her and the guests of honor. What was taking so long? He said a silent prayer that they hadn't run into any trouble along the way from Lennoxville Point.

Just then he heard the *clip-clop, clip-clop* of horse hooves outside and he knew it had to be her. He waited near the door of the tavern to open it and greet her the moment she came in. He was confused to look out the window and see what appeared to be two shadows exiting the carriage. As they came into the light of the lanterns in front of the tavern, his heart sank.

A carriage brought Laney to the tavern, but Charles Jr. wasn't driving it, and she had come with a companion.

It was the very last person Adam would've wanted to see this night.

Francis Smythe.

His past nemesis was now bringing *his* Laney to the gathering—at his family's tavern, no less! As far as he knew, Smythe hadn't set foot in the tavern since the day that he and Adam got into their scuffle just outside the establishment. Smythe walked away from the situation with a broken nose, but the then-seventeen-year-old Adam was sentenced to an apprenticeship.

Why on earth would she think it's a good idea to bring him?

As the pair stepped into the tavern, Adam forced a smile—although no one would've known it was not sincere—and he extended his hand to greet Laney's with a kiss and offered his hand to shake Francis's.

"What a surprise!" Adam said.

Francis nodded nervously and said, "Indeed, I didn't know I was coming here tonight."

Adam looked at Laney with a puzzled expression but spoke as if to both Francis and Laney.

"Is that right? And how did that happen?"

"You'll have to forgive me," said Laney. "If there were any way for me to let you know ahead of time, I'd have certainly done it, but as it is, this was a sort of sudden decision."

Adam looked at the two of them and saw how well put together they both appeared. It certainly didn't look as if their decision to come to the tavern together was extemporaneous. He was at a loss for words.

"I see."

"Well, I must credit Rocksolanah for inviting me. She's so gracious, as always. When I heard she was back in the county, naturally I had to go pay her a visit. When she learned about my father, she was moved. So it was her suggestion that I come to this gathering tonight as a festive distraction."

"Your father?" asked Adam quizzically.

Francis raised his eyebrows, and his eyes grew large in surprise. "You didn't know?"

Adam started to shake his head and he looked at Laney, then back at Francis. "Know… what?"

"My father died over a month ago. I'm alone at the house now, except for the servants, of course."

This was stunning news.

"I hadn't heard," Adam responded. "My deepest sympathies for your loss."

Francis bowed his head in gratitude.

Adam wondered why no one had told him about the death of Ellison Smythe, His Majesty's Customs Agent for Port Beaufort. If he'd been dead a month, he wondered who had taken his place. While it might not've been the most polite thing to do, he decided he'd go ahead and ask.

"I'm so surprised by this news, Francis. Who has taken your father's place? I know he was a man who was greatly respected by many in this town, including my grandfather. I imagine his shoes will be difficult to fill."

Francis nodded. "Indeed. And I feel the weight upon my shoulders even now. I have been selected to serve as interim Customs Agent until the Crown identifies a permanent replacement for the position. It may turn permanent, but as things stand I'm just trying to learn the responsibilities of the job to the best of my ability."

That's why no one told me, he thought. *They know how I feel about Francis Smythe.*

"Well, then," said Adam, "I wish you the best as you find your footing in your new situation."

Francis gave him a nod of gratitude.

What a strange night this is turning out to be.

Adam proceeded to introduce Adam and Laney to the guests they didn't know—Endora, Stela, Aurora, as well as the young ladies accompanying Jackson and Elliot. Finally, Martin and Jenny, the evening's special guests, arrived. After everyone has been introduced, someone suggested Emmanuel say grace before the meal was served.

Emmanuel was seated at one end of the table, Valentine at the other. Boaz was seated across from Mary. Adam was seated across from Endora, and all of the other young men were seated across from their lady companions. Young Aurora had a seat at the corner nearest Emmanuel right beside her grandmother.

Jackson's brothers did a fine job serving all of the guests, but Mary still jumped up a few times to lend a hand—out of habit, no doubt. Even though Adam insisted she just rest and enjoy the meal, it apparently worried her to see half-empty glasses or bread baskets.

While the food was delicious and the music was lively enough that everyone enjoyed dancing after they ate, Adam still couldn't help but feel like the evening hadn't gone quite right. He wasn't sure whether he was angry, sad, or indifferent.

At one point, while some couples were dancing and Valentine was having a turn dancing with the new bride, Martin walked over to Adam and said, "Told you you shoulda said something to Laney. Bet you were surprised to see *that*." He nodded his head in the direction of Laney and Francis dancing.

"Just enjoy your evening," Adam said, annoyed by his friend's comment.

When the gathering ended, Adam stayed behind to help his mother and Jackson's brothers clear the table and clean up. Much to his surprise, Endora insisted that she and her daughters help as well.

"It is the least we can do," she said. "Your family has shown us great hospitality. I am glad that when we leave this town we will be leaving in a better way than we did before."

Mary put her arms around the old woman and gave her a hug. "I wish you didn't have to go," she said.

Adam detected a quaver in his mother's voice. *Is she about to cry?* he wondered.

Endora also embraced Mary. "Ah, sweet girl, I am glad to have had these recent weeks to know you better. You remind me of my own girls. Such a happy free spirit you are."

Adam wasn't too surprised that his mother and Endora had grown close in their short time together. Mary's mother died when she was very young, and she had always been free spirited. He was sad for his mother that she would soon have to say goodbye to the old woman, who had obviously taken her under her wing.

The thing that was surprising to Adam was that it almost seemed now like Endora didn't want to leave. She was making herself right at home in the kitchen of the Topsail Tavern, sharing funny stories about her travels with Mary and Aunt Franny while they took turns washing, drying, and putting away the dishes.

While her mother was busy helping with the dishes, Stela discreetly asked Adam about Ricky Jones as they came in and out from the dining room, putting things back in order. He learned Stela fancied Jones quite a bit, and from what he'd observed at supper, Jones was quite fond of her as well.

He started to wonder if Endora and her daughters really might like to stay in Beaufort. Perhaps he'd mention it to her before helping the ladies get packed and ready to travel back to the gypsy camp near the White Oak River.

He also wanted to talk to Laney, but for now that would have to wait.

Chapter Eleven

FIRST THING MONDAY MORNING, ADAM wasted no time getting ready to go to Laney Martin's estate. Fortunately, Emmanuel had given his workers the day off after the previous day's festivities.

When Adam arrived at her house at Lennoxville Point, he hurriedly tied poor Rex to the hitching post, and he marched up onto the back porch and rang the bell.

He tapped his foot and held his hat as he waited impatiently. Soon, Annabelle answered the door and said, "Good mornin, Mr. Adam. You here to—?"

"I need to see Laney," Adam said.

No sooner had Annabelle stepped out of the way to show him in, he hurried past her and stood in the foyer by the staircase. He had no idea where Laney was, but it made no difference because Laney quickly emerged from the study.

"Adam, what a surprise!"

"We need to talk," he said.

Laney looked startled by his clearly agitated demeanor. She motioned for him to follow her back into the study.

"Have a seat," she said.

"I'll stand, thank you."

"Suit yourself."

After an awkward pause, Laney said, "You seem upset about something."

Adam threw back his head and ran his fingers through his dark, wavy hair in frustration. "Do I really?"

She furrowed her brow at him.

He could see she would soon lose her patience if he didn't get on with whatever it was he wanted to say. He took a deep breath and sighted, then said, "What in the *world* would've given you the idea that it was alright for you to invite *Francis Smythe* of all people to the dinner last night?"

"Adam, I told you that—"

"I know what you told me about his father dying, all of that, but did it not occur to you that I was expecting you to be *my* companion at the supper last night?"

Laney opened her mouth like she was about to speak, but Adam continued before she had a chance. "In case you didn't notice, I was alone last night. I had no one there with me. Martin had his new bride. Jackson was there with Annie. Elliot had Ana. Ricky Jones was there with Stela."

"After seeing her sitting with y'all in church these last few Sundays, I thought she would be with you," Laney said. "I thought there was something between you."

"Of course not! I only ever intended to be there with you. *You.*"

"Adam, I had no idea. I…" She seemed at a loss for words.

"How could you have had no idea? I told you I wanted to bring you myself, but that I would be helping finish up the last few details for the newlyweds. I told you I would send someone for you, but you insisted that Charles Jr. would bring you."

"Adam! Just stop this!" Laney shook her head angrily at

him. "Don't you come in here and start fussing at me like I'm some child! And I'm not your wife! You're in no position to speak to me this way!"

"My position? Of course! I should've known that's what it would come down to." Adam shook his head in disbelief. "You're high society, and I'm just an apprentice for a shipping merchant."

"What?" Laney was visibly flummoxed at his outburst. "I'm not *talking* about your social position, you, you, you... *ridiculous thing*! I'm talking about your position relative to *me*, in that you have expressed no clear"—she seemed to be searching for the right word—"*anything*! All I've ever gotten from you is the occasional flirty smile or boyish charm, but what reason have you given me to think that you consider me as anything other than a friend and occasional shipping associate because of that dock out back?" She thrust her arm out and pointed towards the back of the house.

"How could you be so blind?" he asked her. "I feel like I've made it obvious! And I didn't see the point in making any formal declarations of my feelings for you considering"—he spread out his arms as though he were presenting himself— "again, I'm an apprentice, and I'm bound to my master for another year and three months."

"How dare you ask me how could I be so blind! How could *you* be so blind? I kissed you when you arrived at my brother's house in New Bern. I told you I wanted to know everything about you! If I had been any more forward, it would've been indecent!"

"You kissed my cheek! I did think you had some feelings for me, but that's exactly why I assumed you would have been my companion at the dinner, but no, of all people you

SARA WHITFORD

brought Francis!" He said his name as though merely uttering the word left a bad taste in his mouth. "Francis Smythe! Do you care for him? Are you just weighing your options?"

"Adam Fletcher. You forget I'm two years older than you. Beaufort is hardly a town brimming with suitable bachelors. That doesn't mean that I'm weighing my options, but I can tell you this: there's an old saying—but I'm too much of a lady to say it—but to paraphrase, 'Do _something_ or get off the pot'!"

At that, Adam stood looking at her and took a deep breath. Then, with no warning whatsoever, he crossed the room and stood directly in front of her and gently put both of his hands on her face and leaned down and kissed her right on the mouth. It was a short, sweet kiss, but it was most definitely not on the cheek.

He took a half step back just so he could see her reaction, but her eyes were still closed, so he took that as a sign she didn't mind. He wanted to kiss her again, and it took every bit of self-restraint he had not to, but he kept reminding himself about propriety and not kindling the flames of love until there was a safe place for them to burn.

Finally, after a couple of seconds, she opened her eyes.

"That was fine," she said. "Just fine."

He put his arms around her and held her tight, and she wrapped her arms around him as well. After they had embraced for a moment, he took her by the hand and led her over to the settee by the window so they could sit together.

Once they were seated, he held her delicate hand in his own work-worn hand. He looked her in the eyes and then took a deep breath.

"Laney Martin, you're the only girl I ever think about.

112

It's been that way since the day we met at Richard Rasquelle's party and you were in that dress with the roses. Do you remember?"

She smiled and nodded.

"Gracious, girl! If you knew how often I've dreamt about you..."

She blushed and looked away.

"Listen," he continued, squeezing her hand a little tighter, "the more I've gotten to know you over these last couple of years, the more I realized that I can't imagine life without you."

She looked at him, her eyes suddenly more open.

"But I've also known about the obstacles that are presently in our path—that first of all, I am bound an apprentice until I turn twenty-one, but even when that happens, then what? What will I have to offer you? How can I provide you any security?"

"Adam," she said, shaking her head, "I have everything I could ever need that money could buy, but money can't buy love—and I'd give it all up, anyway, if it meant my future could be with you."

Adam embraced her again. "I'm all yours, sweet girl."

"And my heart belongs to you," she whispered into his ear. She then kissed him just below his ear, and he pulled his head back so he could kiss her properly.

The two shared a moment of tenderness, but as his own emotions began to get carried away, he released her from his embrace and decided he should perhaps lighten the mood.

"You honestly thought I would've gone with the gypsy girl to that dinner?"

Laney laughed and shrugged. "Well..."

"You want to know a funny story?"

She looked at him with curiosity. "Hmm?"

"Well, you know that whole band of gypsies first came to town while you were in Boston. That was when we first met Endora and her granddaughters… Anyway, just so you know, my thoughts were fixed on you even during that time. I dreamt I was floating in the air above this big fancy dance in Boston—because I was just sure you were up there meeting all kinds of high society, eligible young New Englanders—and there you were, dancing. And you were beautiful! But do you know who you were with?"

Laney shook her head. "No, who?"

"Francis Smythe! And to make matters worse, I realized I was hovering above the room in my night shirt!"

Laney laughed in response. "Oh, that's awful!"

"It *was* awful! But it just proves what I was saying: I really have dreamt about you."

"Dancing with Francis Smythe no less."

"Well? So now you can understand why I probably looked like a deer facing a hunter when I saw the two of you together last night."

She squeezed his hand. "Oh, I truly am sorry. I really didn't realize."

"That's alright," he said. "We understand each other now. You know, a few people have been telling me I should have a talk with you about all of this, but I thought it was silly, given the circumstances."

"Oh? So others know about"—she waved her hand back and forth between her and Adam—"this?"

He grinned at her. "A little bit they do. I think for everyone else but you, at least, it's been kind of obvious."

She playfully shoved his shoulder. He pretended to be hurt.

"Listen, Laney… this is important."

She wrinkled her forehead. "What?"

"You know how your cousin is?"

"Martin?"

"Yes. You know how he has been with women? And you might've heard about some of the troubles he's gotten himself into."

She nodded. "Unfortunately, yes."

"Well, I'm not like him. I never had trouble around the fairer sex, but I also have always been taught to treat young ladies with respect, and I think it's just good common sense not to invite trouble."

"What do you mean?"

"I mean, you live on your own—well, except Aunt Celie and her kinfolk, who work here, but your parents aren't living, and your brother doesn't live around here."

Laney looked nervous. "What are you getting at?"

"Ha ha, don't look like that. What I'm trying to say is this: you really do set fires burning"—he tapped on his chest—"in here. So I don't think we should allow ourselves to be led into temptation, or maybe I should more accurately say, *I* need to avoid temptation."

She raised her eyebrows, evidently unsure of what to say.

"I don't reckon I'll be coming over here alone again for a good long while. We can have the whole future together, but not yet. So let's just take things slow, and let's be wise."

She nodded. He thought she understood what he meant, but just to be sure, he said, "Because I'm going to be honest with you, sweet girl. I'm not sure I can handle a year and three months' worth of coming over here and being alone with you without getting myself into trouble."

"I understand."

She stood and motioned that he should stand too. "Let me show you out, then, so you can be on your way."

He followed her to the door that led to the back porch when it occurred to him. "I'm surprised Aunt Celie didn't pop in to check on us."

"Oh," Laney smiled, "she's down over at Cyrus and Violet's cabin helping with their baby, I'm sure. She'll be back soon. I wouldn't be surprised if her nose is itching because we're talking about her right now."

Adam took Laney by the hand and leaned down to kiss her again—on the cheek—before he unhitched Rex and climbed up and rode away. He turned and waved at her once more before taking off like a shot.

ADAM DARTED UP THE STAIRS of the warehouse two at a time until he reached the living quarters. He burst through the door and then closed it exuberantly behind him.

"For heaven's sake, don't take it off the hinges, lad." Emmanuel was sitting in his favorite armchair reading a book, and he looked at Adam up over his spectacles with great curiosity.

Adam crossed the room with a huge grin on his face and rested his hands on the back of the settee.

"Ha! There's only one thing that can explain a face like *that.*" He motioned for his grandson to come around the settee and sit down, which he did.

"Well, you'll be happy to know I finally had a talk with Laney."

"Did you now?" Emmanuel smiled proudly. "Tell me what happened. What did she say? What did *you* say?"

"Oh, there's a lot to it, but long story short, it seems we both have the same hopes for the future." Adam stopped there, and a big smile broke across his cheeks.

Emmanuel raised his eyebrows as if to say, *Go on.*

"I'm going to marry that girl one day." He nodded. "It's just a matter of time."

His grandfather clasped his hands together. "This is the best news I've heard in I can't even remember how long!"

He sat back in a more relaxed fashion before he continued. "She knows I still have a year and three months before my apprenticeship is over, but she also knows I have my own goals I'd like to accomplish before we marry. I'm just thankful there shouldn't be an ugly surprise like the one that happened last night with Francis Smythe."

"That was just a terrible misunderstanding, I'm sure of it."

Adam nodded. "It was, and I mostly blame myself. Everyone has been telling me to just talk to her, but I didn't see the point, since we still have a long while to wait, but now I'm glad I did."

"You know," said Emmanuel, "you're going to need to be very wise about things going forward. The cat's out of the bag now, so you won't be able to rely on just doing things the way you have before when she didn't know."

"Hmph. Believe me, I already thought about that. In fact, you'll be happy to know I told her that, going forward,

I won't likely go out to her estate alone, for the sake of maintaining propriety."

His grandfather nodded. "Very wise. 'The spirit indeed is willing, but the flesh is weak.'"

"You know, one thing I've been thinking about, though," said Adam. "Thursday night is Christmas Eve. This will be Laney's first Christmas without her brother or any other close family nearby. I think we should do something special for her."

"Hmm…" Emmanuel looked pensive. "Indeed, I think we can come up with something special."

Chapter Twelve

INDEED, ADAM AND EMMANUEL DID come up with some-thing to surprise Laney for Christmas.

Over the course of the week, the two of them, along with the other men who worked at Rogers's Shipping Company, planned a great Christmas Eve party for everyone associated with the warehouse and the tavern. They were fortunate to have some feminine input about food and decorations from Mary, Aunt Franny, Endora, her granddaughters, and the new Mrs. Martin Smith.

Valentine initially thought it was silly to have another party so close to the wedding supper they'd had at the tavern on the previous Sunday, but after Adam explained everything to him, he became one of the most enthusiastic participants.

Martin and Jenny would be the ones to covertly get Laney there by insisting that she come celebrate Christmas Eve with them at their house.

Evidently, Martin told her there was a chance they might stop by the warehouse to visit Emmanuel, Adam, and Boaz on Christmas Eve night and he hoped she didn't mind. Of course, he recounted that she seemed more than willing to drop in and pay them a Christmas Eve visit.

Initially Laney had expressed concern about not being

with Aunt Celie for Christmas Eve night, since there had never been a Christmas when they weren't together, but Martin reminded her that this year, with Charles Jr. and Annabelle and all they had recently gone through, she might prefer having a Christmas alone with them.

What Adam had planned, but what Martin *hadn't* told her, was that Aunt Celie and everyone else from the estate would be coming to the warehouse for gift giving after the Christmas Eve supper, but then again Laney didn't know there would be a special supper at the warehouse. As far as she knew, they were just going to be dropping by for a visit.

In addition, the *Gypsy* arrived back at the Rogers's Shipping Company early Tuesday morning, so the crew was fortunately also going to be home for Christmas and able to attend the party as well.

Reverend Miller said he would come, and there was one more guest whom Adam invited, personally, and he surprised even himself by it. Now that he knew Francis Smythe was no rival for Laney's affections, and knowing that this would also be Francis's first Christmas without any living family close by, it seemed inviting him was the right thing to do and entirely in keeping with the Christmas spirit.

By four o'clock on Thursday afternoon, Christmas Eve, the women—with the exception of Jenny—were putting the finishing touches on the warehouse, including boughs of evergreens, candles, decorative wreaths, ribbons, and, of course, a big cluster of mistletoe hanging from the ceiling. Mary had shown them how she turned the place into a party venue by using upturned casks as tables and crates and benches for seating. A couple of long worktables were lined up end to end and draped with tablecloths to make a suitable place for the food to be served.

Aunt Celie, Endora, and her granddaughters were responsible for bringing all of the food from the tavern to the warehouse. The menu for the evening included an array of hors d'oeuvres; for the main course, herbed roast beef with a merlot gravy, mashed potatoes, Yorkshire puddings, green beans, candied carrots, and pickled beets; for dessert, gingerbread, pound cake, fruit cake, eggnog, hot chocolate—and the list went on.

Adam wished he had been able to hire musicians, but all of the ones he knew in town were spending Christmas Eve with their own families and couldn't be bothered to come play for a party. No matter, it should be a full, festive evening regardless, and he happened to personally know there were some decent singers among the guests.

The warehouse was drafty, but fortunately there were two fireplaces lit with lively fires to warm the guests.

By six o'clock everyone had arrived for the supper *except* Martin, Jenny, and Laney. Adam knew they should be arriving any moment, so he stayed close to the door to the warehouse so he could listen.

When he finally heard the *clip-clop, clip-clop* of Whisky and the gravelly sound of cart wheels pulling up outside, his heart pounded in his chest. He couldn't wait to see the look on Laney's face when she came in and realized the surprise. He and Elliot had tacked up burlap over the windows so she wouldn't be able to see the place was illuminated with candles inside, although the usual lanterns were burning outside the entrance. In addition, they had hung some sailcloth across the back half of the warehouse to conceal the dock area *and* to make the front part of the warehouse feel more cozy.

Adam could hear familiar voices outside. He was smiling so hard he thought his cheeks might crack. As soon as the door opened, Laney was talking as she stepped inside.

"Merry Christmas, Miss Laney!" Adam said as he welcomed her to the festivities. "Merry Christmas, Mr. and Mrs. Smith," he said to Martin and Jenny.

Laney's eyes were huge and her mouth agape. She took a deep breath as she looked around the room. "Y'all didn't even tell me about this! I'm not dressed for a party!"

"You look beautiful," Adam whispered to her.

Emmanuel called out from across the room, "Well, now! Everyone's here. Perhaps we can ask Reverend Miller to say grace and enjoy this feast while the food is hot."

Reverend Miller did say a blessing for the meal and the guests, and then Emmanuel invited everyone to serve themselves. They filled their plates and then went back for seconds. Guests seemed to enjoy visiting with one another and were in a festive mood. Adam was surprised to see even Francis Smythe seemed happy. He spotted him sitting at a table and talking to Endora and her younger granddaughter, Aurora, of all people.

After everyone had eaten supper, men who worked at Rogers's Shipping Company cleared everything but the desserts and drinks from the serving tables to make space for presents.

Soon after that, Laney was again surprised when Aunt Celie, Charles Jr., Annabelle, Cyrus, and Violet arrived. Aunt Celie explained that she and her "children" had their own special Christmas supper, but that Mr. Adam wanted them to come to the party as a surprise to her.

On to the gift giving... Emmanuel had one small gift for every guest who attended the party, but as was traditional around Beaufort—and, Adam guessed, probably throughout the colonies—everyone in a superior role would give gifts to those who were in their care or employ, but there were no gifts given in reverse fashion. Parents would give gifts to their children, but children weren't expected to give gifts to their parents. Supervisors gave presents to their workers, masters to their slaves, servants, and apprentices, and so forth. Since the party was a surprise to Laney, Adam had gone ahead and taken the initiative to buy gifts for everyone in her household so they would all have something to open at the party.

After everyone had opened their gifts, Charlie Phillips, the younger brother of the *Gypsy's* captain, Carl Phillips, led everyone in the singing of several Christmas carols, as well as some lively tunes that got many of the folks dancing.

Adam took Laney by the hand and led her out to dance, and he made sure to get her under the mistletoe so he could steal a kiss right in plain view of everyone—not that anyone was paying attention, since everyone who wasn't dancing was in the crowd singing or standing by the punch bowl drinking eggnog or brandy.

When the party ended, Adam noticed Laney shared an embrace with Aunt Celie before Aunt Celie and her own family went back to the Martin estate. The guests started leaving, until the only people left were Adam, Emmanuel, and Boaz, and then Martin, Jenny, and Laney.

Boaz went up to the living quarters first. He said he was ready for a good Christmas sleep with his full belly and a party under his belt. Next, Emmanuel wished the newlyweds a merry Christmas, and Laney too. Then he went upstairs to turn in for the night.

Martin and Jenny said they would go on out to get Whisky and the cart ready to go home, and they left Laney inside to say goodbye to Adam.

Laney and Adam stood near one of the fireplaces before she had to go out of the warehouse for the chilly ride home back to her cousin's house. She and Adam held hands.

"I don't know how to thank you for all of this," she said.

"You don't have to thank me. I couldn't imagine not seeing you for Christmas, but even more, I couldn't imagine you having to be alone at home for Christmas. I'm just glad Martin and Jenny are here and that they helped make all of this happen."

"They really kept a good secret! I honestly thought we might just be stopping by for a quick visit. I had no idea y'all had all of this planned!"

Adam grinned. "I'm happy you enjoyed it."

"I really didn't know how things would be without my brother around. We've never spent Christmas apart. And then I worried about not being with Aunt Celie, because I've always had her with me, all the time, but I understood she might want some time alone with Charles Jr. and his wife."

"I reckon she was worried about not being with you, either. You might not be her child, but I know she's been like a second mama to you. And y'all will see each other tomorrow morning, I'm sure."

Laney smiled and nodded. She looked down, and he thought she might cry.

"Listen," he said, "before you go, I wanted to give you a little something."

She gave him a curious look. "Not a Christmas present?"

Adam shook his head. "No, not quite."

"Well... what is it?"

She looked bright with anticipation, her cheeks rosy from the warmth of the fire.

Adam reached into his pocket and held out a clenched hand; then he opened her palm and placed something inside. She looked down. It was a small silver ring.

Laney raised her eyebrows in astonishment. "What's this?"

"I know this might not be the way to give a lady a ring, to place it in their palm, but I wanted you to be able to see what's engraved on the inside before it goes on your finger, and then once it's on your finger, I hope it will stay there and that it will remind you of my love for you. I wanted you to know that I meant what I said the other night. I was serious."

She gasped as she read the inscription inside the ring.

My heart is yours.

"Oh, Adam!" Her hands trembled as Adam placed it on her finger.

"It's a small thing," he said. "But it means something great to me. I love you."

Laney threw her arms up around his neck and squeezed. "And I love you! I will cherish this ring."

He wrapped his own arms around her back and embraced her tightly. They shared a kiss—this time with no one around—and then he walked her to the door, helped her put on her coat, and he accompanied her outside.

After helping her climb up into the cart with Martin and Jenny, he kissed her hand. "Good night," he said.

"Good night," she said.

"That's all, you lovebirds," said Martin. "We're cold, and it won't be such a good night if we freeze out here in front of the warehouse."

"Thanks for everything," Adam said to Martin.

"My pleasure, ol' friend. I reckon I might owe you one, or two." He laughed.

Adam watched them ride away before he went back inside and up to the living quarters.

His bed by the window in his tiny room was a welcome sight once he made it there. For the first time in quite a while, he finally had something he wanted to write in his journal. After he stripped down to his shirt and breeches, he propped himself up against the wall with a bolster. He pulled the leather journal and pencil out of his dresser drawer and opened to the first blank page he could find.

He didn't have much to write, but he always wanted to remember this...

The 24th of December 1767 Anno Domini

Great Christmas supper here at the warehouse.

I gave Laney a silver ring that says

My heart is yours.

She said she will cherish it, and I cherish her.

I long for the day to make her my Bride.

As always, if you enjoyed *Christmas in Beaufort*, or any of the other Adam Fletcher stories, please take a moment to leave a review.

Thank you!

COLONIAL AMERICAN CHRISTMAS RECIPES & TRIVIA

Some Colonial American Christmas Recipes

THE DISHES MENTIONED ON THE following pages have been enjoyed since colonial times in eastern North Carolina, but they are updated for modern cooking methods. (For instance, there was no such thing as baking soda or baking powder in Colonial America, nor were there electric mixers, and food was cooked by fire rather than at an exact oven temperature.) Many of these might have been enjoyed year-round, but they were especially popular during the Christmas season.

Some of the recipes were graciously contributed by local residents. Others are from the *Southern Living Cookbook* (1995 edition), reprinted with permission from Oxmoor House, Inc. All of them feature a bit of commentary from me, the author of this book.

Roasted Duck
134

Venison and Gravy
136

Clam Chowder with Cornmeal Dumplings
138

Candied Sweet Potatoes
140

Holiday Eggnog
142

Wassail
144

Raisin-Nut Cake with Brown Sugar Glaze
146

Old-Fashioned Gingerbread
148

Molasses Cake
150

Buttermilk Pound Cake
152

And a contemporary favorite...
Layered Coconut Cake
154

Roasted Duck

BASIC RECIPE. MODIFY SPICES AS YOU DESIRE.

SOME LOCAL HISTORY

Mr. Austin Guthrie, whose family has lived along Bogue Banks since the 1700s, recalls black duck or Mallard being a special treat at Christmastime for his family. In particular, he remembers his father selling ducks back in the 1930s and '40s for a dollar a pair to local doctors and lawyers during the holiday season. If there were any ducks left over after selling as many as they could, then his family would have whatever was remaining for Christmas dinner. Otherwise, they had boiled ham. The Guthries of Cedar Point continue to be avid duck hunters to this day.

INGREDIENTS

1 (5-pound) whole duck (innards and wing tips removed)

1 ½ teaspoons salt

2 teaspoons paprika

1 teaspoon garlic powder (optional)

1 teaspoon black pepper

½ stick melted butter (for basting, optional)

1 onion, quartered

3 sprigs fresh thyme

INSTRUCTIONS

Preheat oven to 375º. Combine salt, paprika, garlic powder, and black pepper and rub well all over duck, and also sprinkle some inside cavity. Stuff cavity with quartered onion and thyme. Place seasoned, stuffed duck in roasting pan and roast in preheated oven for about one hour. Baste with juices from duck, or if you prefer, you can use melted butter. Continue to cook for another half hour and baste again. After another 20 minutes or so, begin checking internal temperature at thickest part of thigh for doneness. Meat thermometer should register at about 165-170º.

Venison and Gravy

RECIPE COURTESY OF JUDY WEST LINEBARGER
OF CARTERET COUNTY.

SOME LOCAL HISTORY

Judy West Linebarger and her husband, Jerry Linebarger are both descendants of the Garner family of Carteret County on their maternal lines. The Garner family has lived along Bogue Sound since the 1700s. Because this recipe has been passed down by word of mouth in Judy's family, there are no exact measurements. On the bright side, this just means you can easily scale the recipe as needed for your particular crowd. Jerry Linebarger remembers hunting back when it was a necessary means of putting food on the table. He said that back then you often hunted as a group and whatever was killed was divided up – usually with an axe. An old Newport hunter used to say, "What ain't on one side'll be on t'other."

INGREDIENTS

Several thinly-sliced venison steaks, trimmed of fat
All-purpose flour
Lard
2 cups (roughly) water
Salt and pepper

INSTRUCTIONS

Sprinkle venison steaks as desired with salt and pepper. Dredge in flour, then pan fry in thin layer of lard until steaks are brown.

Remove steaks from pan, leaving grease and bits from frying. Add about 3 or 4 more Tablespoons of flour to the pan and brown. Add water, then bring to a boil.

Return steaks to gravy and simmer until meat is tender. Add salt and pepper to taste. Serve with rice.

Clam Chowder
with Cornmeal Dumplings

THIS BROTH-STYLE CHOWDER IS A CARTERET COUNTY
FAVORITE, WITH OR WITHOUT THE DUMPLINGS.

DUMPLINGS VS. PASTRY

To this day, in eastern North Carolina, dumplings are understood to be something completely different from the flour-based pastry that often accompanies stewed chicken. (For instance, Cracker Barrel restaurants serve "Chicken and Dumplins," but what they refer to as "Dumplins" are actually what we refer to as "pastry." In eastern North Carolina, dumplings are made with cornmeal, salt, and water, whereas pastry is made with flour, salt, and water. Either can be used in a variety of ways, such as with: chicken, squirrel, rabbit, or clams. There is one dish that only lends itself to dumplings and not pastry: collard greens.

CHOWDER INGREDIENTS

3-4 cups of clams, cleaned well and diced
1 large piece streak of lean
5 white or red potatoes, peeled and cubed
1 large onion, diced
Salt and pepper, to taste

DUMPLING INGREDIENTS

2 cups corn meal
Salt, to taste
Water

INSTRUCTIONS

Boil salt pork in a stockpot until the meat is tender, about 1 hour. Add diced clams, cubed potatoes, and diced onion and boil for about 30 minutes or so. You will want to taste for saltiness. It may be that the streak of lean has salted the potatoes plenty, but if not, add additional salt to taste.

In a separate bowl, mix corn meal, water, and salt to taste until you have a dough that can be formed into dumplings. Drop into chowder and boil during the last 15-20 minutes of cooking.

Candied Sweet Potatoes

ONE VERSION OF A PERSONAL FAMILY RECIPE.

VERSATILE SWEET POTATOES

We southerners sure do love our sweet potatoes. They can be enjoyed sweet or savory, and prepared in so many different ways. These days, if you have Thanksgiving or Christmas dinner with an eastern North Carolina family, you're more likely to see a Sweet Potato Casserole topped with marshmallows (a dish typically referred to in my own family as "Sweet Potato Fluff") than you are to see the old-fashioned Candied Sweet Potatoes (or what is often marketed as "candied yams," nevermind that yams and sweet potatoes aren't exactly the same thing). Nevertheless, Candied Sweet Potatoes would've been what was likely served before the advent of the big, fluffy, white marshmallows, which didn't come along until the 1800s.

INGREDIENTS

Baked sweet potatoes (about 6 to 8 small or medium sweet
potatoes, or 3 or 4 large sweet potatoes)

Cinnamon

1 cup white sugar

1 cup brown sugar*

1 stick of butter

¼ cup water

¼ teaspoon salt

INSTRUCTIONS

Preheat oven to 400º. Remove baked sweet potatoes from
skins. Cut into pieces of desired size and place in baking dish.

Sprinkle sweet potato pieces with cinnamon.

In a pot over medium heat, make a syrup of the brown sugar,
butter, and salt, then pour over sweet potatoes. Bake in 400º
oven for about 35 minutes.

* *If you don't have brown sugar on hand, you can substitute another cup
of white sugar and a teaspoon or a tablespoon of molasses, depending on
whether you prefer light brown or dark brown sugar.*

Holiday Eggnog

FROM *THE SOUTHERN LIVING COOKBOOK*
YIELD: 2 QUARTS

THE OLD-FASHIONED WAY

When one of my older relatives told me how she had always made egg nog, there was no cooking involved. "The liquor makes it keep," she said. I believe it. Traditional eggnog recipes wouldn't have involved cooking the yolks before adding other ingredients, in fact, I can just imagine Adam and Mary and Valentine and Emmanuel laughing at all of us for doing any such thing, but since I'd rather not get sued in case a reader gets sick from bad eggs, I'm going to stick with sharing this "safe" recipe from a favorite cookbook. If you'd like to walk on the wild side and make some old-school eggnog, you can find plenty of those recipes online.

INGREDIENTS

6 egg yolks

1 cup sugar

½ teaspoon vanilla extract

¼ teaspoon ground nutmeg

2 cups milk

¾ cup brandy

¼ cup rum

1 cup heavy cream

2 cups whipping cream, whipped

Ground nutmeg (for garnish)

INSTRUCTIONS

Beat egg yolks until thick and lemon colored; gradually add 1 cup sugar, vanilla, and ¼ teaspoon nutmeg, beating well at medium speed of an electric mixer. Place milk in a heavy saucepan over medium-low heat. Gradually add egg yolk mixture; cook, stirring constantly with a wire whisk, until mixture reaches 160° (about 30 minutes). Remove from heat; let cool. Stir in brandy, rum, and 1 cup whipping cream. Cover and chill 8 hours.

Place chilled mixture in a punch bowl. Fold whipped cream into chilled mixture. Sprinkle with nutmeg.

Wassail

FROM *THE SOUTHERN LIVING COOKBOOK*
YIELD: 3 QUARTS

A VERY OLD TRADITION

The following is a bit of history from Merriam-Webster.com:

"The salutation wassail, from the Old Norse toast *ves heill* ("be well"), has accompanied English toast-making since the 12th century. By the 13th century, wassail was being used for the drink itself, and it eventually came to be used especially of a hot drink (of wine, beer, or cider with spices, sugar, and usually baked apples) drunk around Christmastime. This beverage warmed the stomachs and hearts of many Christmas revelers and was often shared with Christmas carolers. The verb wassail was first used in the 14th century to describe the carousing associated with indulgence in the drink; later, it was used of other activities associated with wassail and the holiday season, like caroling. Seventeenth-century farmers added cattle and trees to the wassail tradition by drinking to their health or vitality during wintertime festivities."

In spite of its "spirited" history, this version of the centuries-old Christmas drink is one the children can enjoy.

INGREDIENTS

2 quarts apple juice

2 ¼ cups pineapple juice

2 cups orange juice

1 cup lemon juice

½ cup sugar

1 (3-inch) stick cinnamon

1 teaspoon whole cloves

INSTRUCTIONS

Combine all ingredients in a Dutch oven; bring to a boil. Cover, reduce heat, and simmer 20 minutes. Uncover and simmer an additional 20 minutes. Strain and discard cinnamon and cloves. Serve hot.

Raisin-Nut Cake with Brown Sugar Glaze

FROM *THE SOUTHERN LIVING COOKBOOK*

A FRUIT AND NUT CAKE

Regardless of what you think about them, a fruit cake seems like a must in a list of Christmas recipes.

CAKE INGREDIENTS

1 cup raisins

½ cup bourbon

1 cup butter, softened

2 ¼ cups sugar

5 eggs

3 ¼ cups all-purpose flour

1 teaspoon baking powder

½ teaspoon baking soda

1 ½ teaspoons ground nutmeg

1 cup buttermilk

2 cups coarsely chopped pecans

BROWN SUGAR GLAZE INGREDIENTS
(YIELD: 2/3 CUP)

½ cup firmly packed light brown sugar
½ cup butter
¼ cup milk

CAKE INSTRUCTIONS

Combine raisins and bourbon, stirring well. Cover and refrigerate at least 1 hour. Cream butter; gradually add sugar, beating well at medium speed of an electric mixer. Add eggs, one at a time, beating well after each addition.

Combine flour, baking powder, soda, and nutmeg; add to creamed mixture alternately with buttermilk, beginning and ending with flour mixture. Mix after each addition. Fold in pecans and reserved raisin mixture.

Pour batter into a greased and floured 10-inch tube pan. Bake at 325° for 1 hour and 30 minutes or until a wooden toothpick inserted in center comes out clean. Cool in pan 10 minutes; remove from pan and place on serving plate.

BROWN SUGAR GLAZE INSTRUCTIONS

Combine ½ cup firmly packed light brown sugar, ½ cup butter, and ¼ cup milk in a heavy saucepan; bring to a full boil and cook, stirring constantly, 2 minutes. Let cool to lukewarm. Drizzle Brown Sugar Glaze over cake. Cool completely.

Old-Fashioned Gingerbread

FROM *THE SOUTHERN LIVING COOKBOOK*
YIELD: 9 SERVINGS

THE CAKE, NOT THE COOKIES

Aside from ginger, one of the key ingredients to Gingerbread —whether we're talking about cake *or* cookies— is molasses. That probably explains why some people think Gingerbread and Molasses Cake are the same thing, and for some people, they may be. In my own family, however, they are two different cakes. Gingerbread cake has more spice than it's cousin, Molasses Cake. As such, I'm including both recipes here. Gingerbread is a very Christmasy recipe, whereas Molasses Cake might have been enjoyed year-round. (A Molasses Cake recipe can be found on the page after this one.)

INGREDIENTS

½ cup butter, softened

½ cup sugar

1 egg

1 cup molasses

2 ½ cups all-purpose flour

1 ½ teaspoons baking soda

½ teaspoon salt

1 teaspoon ground cinnamon

1 teaspoon ground cloves

1 teaspoon ground ginger

1 cup hot water

Sweetened whipped cream

INSTRUCTIONS

Cream butter; gradually add sugar, beating at medium speed of an electric mixer until light and fluffy. Add egg and molasses, mixing well.

Combine flour and next 5 ingredients; add to creamed mixture alternately with water, beginning and ending with flour mixture. Mix after each addition.

Pour batter into a lightly greased and floured 9-inch square pan. Bake at 350° for 35 to 40 minutes or until a wooden toothpick inserted in center comes out clean. Serve with a dollop of whipped cream.

Molasses Cake

THIS IS SIMILAR TO THE GINGERBREAD CAKE RECIPE,
BUT IT CUTS THE CINNAMON AND GINGER IN HALF,
AND IT OMITS THE CLOVES.

ALMOST EXACTLY LIKE AUNT FRANNY'S

Let's face it. Aunt Franny doesn't measure things and she doesn't follow written recipes, or "receipts," as they would've been called in her day. She just *knows* how to make things that taste delicious. I have it on good authority, though, that this recipe is remarkably like hers.

ONE TIP: *NEVER* use Blackstrap Molasses for baking unless the recipe *specifically* calls for it. It's the complete wrong thing. Just use regular, good old-fashioned molasses. Personally, I'm a fan of the Grandma's Molasses brand, but there are many other good options out there, I'm sure.

INGREDIENTS

½ cup butter, softened

½ cup sugar

1 egg

1 cup molasses

2 ½ cups all-purpose flour

1 ½ teaspoons baking soda

½ teaspoon salt

½ teaspoon ground cinnamon

½ teaspoon ground ginger

1 cup hot water

Sweetened whipped cream

INSTRUCTIONS

Cream butter; gradually add sugar, beating at medium speed of an electric mixer until light and fluffy. Add egg and molasses, mixing well.

Combine flour and next 4 ingredients; add to creamed mixture alternately with water, beginning and ending with flour mixture. Mix after each addition.

Pour batter into a lightly greased and floured 9-inch square pan. Bake at 350º for 35 to 40 minutes or until a wooden toothpick inserted in center comes out clean. Serve with a dollop of whipped cream.

Buttermilk Pound Cake

MODIFIED FROM *THE SOUTHERN LIVING COOKBOOK*

HAVE YOU EVER SEEN A COLONIAL-ERA POUND CAKE RECIPE?

Goodness gracious! Usually recipes for eighteenth century pound cakes called for a pound of flour, a pound of eggs, a pound of butter, and a pound of sugar, and then a variety of other flavorings and ingredients. In other words, when all was said and done, you'd wind up with an almost five-pound cake! Personally, a good old-fashioned pound cake is one of my very favorite desserts —I don't care if it's Christmas or just some random Wednesday. The recipe that follows is a modified version of *The Southern Living Cookbook*'s Buttermilk Pound Cake recipe. It's my go-to, although I'll admit I sometimes do all kinds of different things with the flavorings and extracts.

INGREDIENTS

1 cup butter, softened

2 cups sugar

4 eggs

½ teaspoon baking soda

1 cup buttermilk

3 cups all-purpose flour

1/8 teaspoon salt

2 teaspoons brandy, or rum, or lemon extract, whichever
you prefer

1 teaspoon vanilla extract

INSTRUCTIONS

Cream butter; gradually add sugar, beating well at medium speed of an electric mixer. Add eggs, one at a time, beating after each addition.

Dissolve soda in buttermilk. Combine flour and salt; add to creamed mixture alternately with buttermilk, beginning and ending with flour mixture. Mix just until blended after each addition. Stir in flavorings.

Pour batter into greased 10-inch tube pan and bake at 350° for about an hour. Cake is done when inserted wooden toothpick comes out clean. Cool in pan 10 to 15 minutes; remove from pan and let cool completely on a wire rack. (*Note: Cake may also be baked in two 9- x 5- x 3-inch loaf pans, but reduce cooking time by about 15 minutes.*)

Layered Coconut Cake

A MODIFIED VERSION OF A BASIC
CONTEMPORARY RECIPE.

SOME LOCAL HISTORY

In eastern North Carolina, one especially beloved dessert has long been the Coconut Layer Cake. Mary Toler Collins of Maysville, North Carolina, remembers as a young girl that her mother's Christmastime coconut cake recipe required her to purchase a whole coconut, special ordered, from the grocer. Mary said shredded coconut wasn't available in Jones County in those days. Her father would have to carefully split the coconut and shred the coconut flesh by hand. The liquid was reserved for part of the recipe.

While the following recipe isn't the one that was used by Mary's mother, it's just one of many versions of our cherished Coconut Layer Cake, and in true contemporary style, it even uses a boxed mix and an uncooked frosting for simplicity's sake.

INGREDIENTS

1 box cake mix (white or yellow is fine), prepared as directed
and baked in two 9-inch round cake pans. Once cake has
cooled, cut each round in half horizontally so that you have
four layers altogether.

2 cups sour cream

2 cups sugar

2 packages of fresh, frozen coconut (6 oz. packages)

1 ½ cups heavy whipping cream

FILLING INSTRUCTIONS

Combine sour cream and sugar, then add 1 ½ packages of
coconut. (Reserve ½ package of coconut for garnish on finished cake.) Filling will be very soft. Reserve one cup of filling
mixture to combine with whipping cream for frosting.

Assemble cake, one layer at a time, with filling in between
each layer. If you'd like, you can refrigerate cake to firm everything up before frosting.

FROSTING INSTRUCTIONS

Use electric mixer on medium speed to whip heavy cream
until stiff peaks form. Fold in filling mixture and mix well
with spoon. Frost cake, then top with remaining fresh
shredded coconut as garnish.

Colonial American
Christmas Trivia

I've come across many interesting facts while doing research over the years. Here are a few relating to Christmas in eastern North Carolina, and throughout Colonial America.

- In North Carolina, and throughout Colonial America, Christmas was first and foremost a religious holiday focused on the birth of Jesus Christ, but that doesn't mean it was treated as a "day off" as it is today.

- In many parts of early Colonial America, no feasts or parties were held to mark Christmas, as some viewed such celebrations as pagan.

- After the Revolutionary War, Congress held its first session on Christmas Day of 1789.

- The indulgent Christmas beverage known as eggnog is a descendant of a much older drink called posset, which dates back to the fourteenth century. Posset was enjoyed hot, and its recipes didn't call for eggs, but rather they were a concoction of curdled milk and wine or ale.

- It's been reported that Captain John Smith was the first person to make a type of eggnog in America. It happened at Jamestown on Christmas 1607.

- On Christmas Day in 1739, famed evangelist George Whitefield preached at the courthouse at New Bern.

- As is mentioned in *Christmas in Beaufort*, gift-giving was not practiced in the eighteenth century the way that it is today. According to historian Emma L. Powers[1]: "Williamsburg shopkeepers of the eighteenth century placed ads noting items appropriate as holiday gifts… Cash tips, little books, and sweets in small quantities were given by masters or parents to dependents, whether slaves, servants, apprentices, or children. It seems to have worked in only one direction: children and others did not give gifts to their superiors."

- The secularized Santa Claus figure of today would be totally unrecognizable in Colonial America, a fact that shouldn't be surprising considering contemporary images of Ol' St. Nick were inspired by Clement Clark Moore's poem "A Visit by Saint Nicholas," which wasn't published until December 23, 1823. (The real basis for Saint Nicholas was a fourth century Christian bishop known as Nicholas of Myra, who from the ancient Greek city of Myra in Asia Minor, or what is today known as Demre, Turkey. According to the Green Orthodox church, Nicholas "is the patron of all travellers, and of sea-farers in particular; he is one of the best known and best loved Saints of all time."

- Although a variety of fruits often figure into the designs of wreaths and other Christmas décor at favorite colonial tourist spots like New Bern's Tryon Palace or Colonial Williamsburg, according to historians working at those locations, such pricey and seasonally difficult-to-obtain items would never have been used to hang from doors and windows.

- There are no definitive written sources about typical Christmas décor in the colonial era, but from illustrations that were made at the time, greenery appears to have been used, but mistletoe figured most prominently in festive designs.

- November, December, and January were the most popular months for weddings in the colonial era[2], so a Christmas wedding, like Martin and Jenny's would've been right in line with what was typical at that time. This had as much to do with practical considerations as anything, since farming and other season-dependent work would've made weddings during warmer months inconvenient, or downright impossible.

- While contemporary American Christmas focuses only on Christmas Eve and Christmas Day (retailers notwithstanding), Colonial Americans saw the Christmas season as a full twelve days, hence the famous song, "The Twelve Days of Christmas."

- Twelfth Night took place on January 5, the eve of Epiphany, the day when some believe the nativity story places the wise men visiting the newborn baby Jesus.

- In many countries in Europe and Latin America, January 6 is still celebrated as the culmination of the year's Christmas observances.

- Residents of Hatteras Island still celebrate what is referred to as "Old Christmas" or "Little Christmas" on January 5 and 6 at Rodanthe. According to historian Wynne Dough[3], the tradition, "resulted from the adoption of the Gregorian calendar by the British Empire in 1752. Scattered parts of the American colonies refused to celebrate Christmas on the new date (25 December) and eventually merged Old Christmas into the New Epiphany (6 January), creating a joint observance not seen in the West since the fourth century. … In time, 25 December became the focus of religious sentiment, and Old Christmas turned secular."

- If you're in the mood to celebrate a Colonial American Christmas, you should make plans to visit the Candlelight Christmas Celebration at Tryon Palace in New Bern or work in a trip to Colonial Williamsburg.

[1] "Colonial Christmas Customs" by Emma L. Powers. *The Colonial Williamsburg Interpreter*, Winter 1995-96.

[2] "Courtship and Marriage in the Eighteenth Century" by Elizabeth Maurer. *The Colonial Williamsburg Interpreter*, Winter 1997.

[3] "Old Christmas" by Wynne Dough. *Encyclopedia of North Carolina*, 2006. Edited by William S. Powell.

Acknowledgements

AS ALWAYS, I THANK GOD FIRST, for allowing me to continue writing and publishing, and especially for helping me get this book out before the end of 2018. There were some setbacks along the way, but everything came together. I thank my son, Isaac, for his constant encouragement when I'm in intense writing mode, or when I'm struggling to find any words to write at all. I'm thankful to my sweet mama, Teresa, my sister-in-law, Mallori Guthrie Morris, and my dear friend, Lori Vinskus, for helping me round up some recipes with regional roots. I also want to thank Beaufort artist and historian, Mary Faith Warshaw, for helping me solve a couple of puzzles about traveling in Carteret County in the 1760s. A very special thank you to my good friend and fellow author Terrance Zepke, who has been after me to write some sort of Christmas short story or novella almost since I started writing the Adam Fletcher books. It's entirely possible that without her insistence that I do this, it might never have happened. Mom, I know you're reading this... You've been after me, too, to write something that's not just an adventure. I hope this story passes the test. :) Finally, as you all already know, I thank you, my readers, for your support and enthusiasm for Adam Fletcher and his adventures. Keep reading, because there is much more in store!

A Record of the Birth of Christ

from the Gospel of Luke (KJV)

And it came to pass in those days, that there went out a decree from Cæsar Augustus, that all the world should be taxed. (And this taxing was first made when Cyrenius was governor of Syria.) And all went to be taxed, every one into his own city. And Joseph also went up from Galilee, out of the city of Nazareth, into Judæa, unto the city of David, which is called Bethlehem; (because he was of the house and lineage of David:) to be taxed with Mary his espoused wife, being great with child.

And so it was, that, while they were there, the days were accomplished that she should be delivered. And she brought forth her firstborn son, and wrapped him in swaddling clothes, and laid him in a manger; because there was no room for them in the inn.

And there were in the same country shepherds abiding in the field, keeping watch over their flock by night. And, lo, the angel of the Lord came upon them, and the glory of the Lord shone round about them: and they were sore afraid.

And the angel said unto them, Fear not: for, behold, I bring you good tidings of great joy, which shall be to all people. For unto you is born this day in the city of David a Saviour, which is Christ the Lord. And this shall be a sign unto you; Ye shall find the babe wrapped in swaddling clothes, lying in a manger. And suddenly there was with the angel a multitude of the heavenly host praising God, and saying, Glory to God in the highest, and on earth peace, good will toward men.

And it came to pass, as the angels were gone away from them into heaven, the shepherds said one to another, Let us now go even unto Bethlehem, and see this thing which is come to pass, which the Lord hath made known unto us. And they came with haste, and found Mary, and Joseph, and the babe lying in a manger. And when they had seen it, they made known abroad the saying which was told them concerning this child. And all they that heard it wondered at those things which were told them by the shepherds. But Mary kept all these things, and pondered them in her heart. And the shepherds returned, glorifying and praising God for all the things that they had heard and seen, as it was told unto them.

(*Luke* 2:1-20)

SIGN UP FOR
THE GAZETTE
FOR BOOK UPDATES AND
SPECIAL DISCOUNTS.

Go to AdamFletcherSeries.com/subscribe

*Wishing you a very
Merry Christmas from the entire
Adam Fletcher Adventure Series
family. May God bless you and
yours this holiday season and
in the years to come.*

Have you read all of Adam Fletcher's Adventures?

More titles are forthcoming.

Subscribe to THE GAZETTE *newsletter at*
AdamFletcherSeries.com/subscribe *for updates.*